LEON STUMBLE'S BOOK OF STUPID FAIRYTALES

Doug MacLeod • Craig Smith

working title press

For Jane and Sue. And Sister Madge Mappin.

The illustrations in this book are drawn with a nib, an old brush, and charcoal pencil. The cover was coloured in Painter 8 software.

Working Title Press
ABN 29 076 867 751
33 Balham Avenue
Kingswood SA 5062

First published 2005

Text copyright © Estuary Productions 2005
Illustrations copyright © Craig Smith 2005

Scanning of artwork by Skanz, Adelaide
Typeset in Worcester and Latino by Patricia Howes
Printed in China by SNP Leefung Printers Ltd
Distributed by Scholastic Australia Pty Ltd
(02) 4328 3555

All rights reserved

National Library of Australia Cataloguing-in-Publication entry

MacLeod, Doug, 1805- .
Leon Stumble's book of stupid fairytales.

For primary school students.
ISBN 1 876288 66 3 (pbk.).

I. Smith, Craig, 1955- . II. Title.

A823.3

Contents

How it all started	1
Jack and the Branstalk	11
Cinderolla	29
Puss in Blots	47
Little Reg Riding Hood	63
The Princess and the Peg	77
What happened next	95
The Sappy Prince	107
The Gingerbread Mane	129
Goldilocks and The Three Beards	143
Pansel and Grekel	159
Snow White and the Seventy Dwarfs	175
How it all ended	203

How it all started

Dear Leon Stumble,

I'm afraid we cannot publish your children's book, The History of Paste. *I will be as polite as I can. It's dreadful. I tried reading it out to a group of schoolchildren. They offered me money to stop. I took it but still felt bad.*

I see that this is the tenth time you have tried to write a children's book for the Honeybump Publishing Company. Your first attempt was Fun with Coal. *I thought it was impossible to make coal more boring than it is, but somehow you managed. And no, it wouldn't work as a pop-up. People don't want lumps of coal popping up in their faces.*

Your next effort was Interesting Things To Do With Your Arm. *Not one of the things you listed was interesting. Two of them were actually dangerous. I took your work home to line my cat's litter box. She then refused to use it, so I buried your pages in the garden. Nothing has grown there since.*

Mr Stumble, your problem is that you choose boring things to write about. Exciting Turkey *was the worst. There is nothing exciting about a farmyard fowl. Until you can think of some more interesting subjects, please stop bothering us. I'm afraid I cannot return your latest work, as the mice ate it. They got food poisoning.*

Yours sincerely,
Una Spooner
(Publisher)

Leon Stumble had a lot of things going for him. He was young, bright and handsome, and he had a wonderful girlfriend. But Leon wasn't totally happy. More than anything he wanted to be a children's writer, but it didn't seem to be working out.

He tossed the cruel letter from Una Spooner into the bin.

If Leon hadn't been so busy trying to think of educational things to write about, he might have guessed that something strange was going on. Whatever Leon threw, the bin slid around to catch it. Leon didn't notice.

Leon's girlfriend was called Cassie. Like Leon, Cassie was young and good-looking, but unlike Leon, she believed in magic. (Leon thought magic was utter rubbish.) However, Leon and Cassie got on well. They took turns to make dinner for each other, even though neither could cook. Leon would burn the food on Monday night and Cassie would burn it on Tuesday night. They enjoyed walking along the beach. They enjoyed movies. They didn't enjoy pianos falling on their heads, but fortunately this never happened. Life as a couple seemed fairly good, even if Leon couldn't get his books published.

Eventually Cassie thought it might be an idea for her and Leon to get married, but there was one slight problem. Cassie was a witch. She was a very pleasant sort of witch. She didn't have a nose like a carrot or eat toads or anything like that. Nevertheless, she was a witch, and Leon didn't know.

Witches have certain rules. The main one is that you're not allowed to tell ordinary people that you're a witch. If you're at a party and someone asks you what you do for a living, you mustn't reply, 'I'm a witch. What do you do?' You have to make up something else. That was why when Cassie first met Leon at a party she told him that she was an aerobics teacher.

It's quite all right for people to *guess* that you're a witch. If someone says, 'Hang on, you're hovering off the ground, and aerobics teachers don't normally do that. You're actually a witch, aren't you?', then you are allowed to nod and reveal the truth about yourself. But in the six months they'd been together, Leon had been too caught up in trying to write educational children's books to guess the truth about Cassie.

'Leon, I wonder if you've noticed anything *unusual* about me?' asked Cassie one night.

'Bother!' said Leon. His computer had just frozen. The latest book he was writing was called *How Computers Work*. Even Leon had his doubts that this was a good title since it's obvious that most computers don't work at all.

'You haven't noticed anything special about the way I do the cooking?' continued Cassie, snapping her fingers softly behind her back and causing a sausage to explode in the kitchen.

'Not really,' said Leon. 'You've been exploding quite a few sausages lately, but I have the same problem when *I* cook them. Perhaps I should write an educational book about the correct way to cook sausages?'

It seemed that Leon wasn't going to pick up on any of Cassie's hints.

'I think you should stop writing educational books for a little while,' said Cassie, sitting in her favourite armchair, which floated slightly above the ground, 'and write fairytales.'

'I hate fairytales,' said Leon. 'Why would I write a book like that?'

'Because then you would discover there is *magic* in the world,' said Cassie. (And if Leon discovered there was magic in the world, he might notice that his girlfriend was a witch!) 'You could also earn some money,' she added. 'You might even impress that Una Spooner!'

'I don't think anything would impress Una Spooner,' said Leon sadly.

It might seem strange that a witch should be worried about money. But true witches are not allowed to use their magic for personal gain. They can use it to prevent floods or do the vacuuming, but they can't just conjure up piles of money. It's another one of those fiddly witch rules.

'I'm sorry I don't earn much money,' said Leon. 'Perhaps they could pay you more to teach aerobics classes on Wednesday nights?'

Cassie didn't actually teach aerobics classes on Wednesday nights. Instead, she secretly flew to the planet Venus for a few hours to catch up with her witch friends and discuss interesting new spells. But of course she couldn't tell Leon that. The temperature on the surface of Venus is 470°C, so Cassie always came back sweating and with her clothes slightly melted. Leon just assumed she was teaching very energetic aerobics.

At one of these meetings, Cassie had complained to another witch about Leon.

'He's not a bad person,' she said to a little old lady with one purple eye and one green one, 'except he's so unobservant. Honestly, he wouldn't know if his bottom was on fire.'

'He's just a bit distracted,' said the little old lady. 'It can happen to anyone. By the way, your bottom's on fire.'

Leon booted up his computer again. 'What good are fairytales?' he muttered.

'The ones I know are *very* good,' said Cassie.

She sat at Leon's computer and typed the titles of all the fairytales she knew. There were favourites like *Jack and the Beanstalk* and *The Princess and the Pea* and, of course, *Cinderella*.

'Everyone knows those fairytales!' scoffed Leon. 'What would be the point of writing them all over again?'

Then a surprising thing happened. Some of the letters in the titles changed. *Beanstalk* became *Branstalk*. *Cinderella* became *Cinderolla*.

'It must be magic,' said Cassie, with a twinkle in her eye.

'It's a computer virus,' said Leon.

'Well, now you have brand new titles, so you can write brand new fairytales!' said Cassie.

Leon stared at Cassie for a moment. There did seem to be something unusual about her. 'Cassie,' he said, 'you're not really an aerobics teacher, are you?'

Cassie was so excited that her armchair spun around. Leon was going to ask her if she was a witch! 'No, I'm not an aerobics teacher.'

'You're a *librarian*, aren't you?' said Leon.

'What?' Cassie looked angry.

'Well, you know, the whole idea of a book of fairytales with silly titles ...'

'I am *not* a librarian!'

'I wouldn't mind if you were,' said Leon. 'I like librarians.'

Cassie left the room in a huff. If Leon had been more observant he would have noticed that her armchair followed her. But he wasn't observant. He was a writer. And so, to cheer up Cassie, Leon sat down at his keyboard and started typing the amazing story of *Jack and the Branstalk*.

Jack and the Branstalk

Once upon a time there was a poor old widow who had an only son named Jack, who was a vegetarian. Jack had made a vow that he would never eat anything with a face. He dreamed that one day he would run a health food shop that sold nuts and carob and that weird grass stuff.

In the meantime, all Jack and the widow had to live on was the milk their cow gave every morning.

'Pansy is our beloved cow and we owe our lives to her!' said the widow.

Then one morning the cow stopped giving milk.

'Pansy is a stupid old cow and we will eat her!' said the widow.

'No, Mother,' said Jack. 'I am a vegetarian, and I cannot eat anything with a face.'

'Then I'll eat the front half and you can have the back,' said the widow. 'There's no face on that.'

'I cannot eat any part of dear old Pansy,' said Jack. 'And I forbid you to as well.'

'Then what will we eat?' demanded the widow. 'Bricks? Candles? Thermal underwear?'

'Let me take the cow,' said Jack. 'I will sell her, and with the money I will buy vegetarian food for us both.'

'But surely the person who buys her will want to eat her anyway? So why don't we just eat her ourselves?'

'I will sell her to a circus,' said Jack. 'I have been teaching her tricks. Show Mother your special trick, Pansy!'

Pansy did some poo.

'Is that the trick?' asked the widow.

'No,' said Jack. 'I have taught her to balance a chair on her nose.'

Jack handed a chair to Pansy. She looked at it for a few moments and then did some poo on that as well.

'People do not go to circuses to see things like

that,' said the widow, 'unless they have very boring lives.'

'Please let me try to sell her, Mother!' said Jack.

'Pah! On your way then!' said the widow.

Jack took Pansy's halter in his hand, and off he headed to find a circus that would buy her.

His empty tummy was rumbling badly. He walked past an apple orchard and gazed longingly at the red fruit hanging from the trees. Now, Jack was an honest boy, but he was so hungry that he decided he would have to steal some of the apples and gobble them down. However, the farmer had suspected Jack might try this and, knowing Jack was a vegetarian, he had drawn faces on all the apples so Jack couldn't eat a single one.

Before long he met a funny-looking old man who said to him, 'Where are you going with that cow?'

'I am searching for a circus that will buy her!' said Jack.

'Now, isn't that strange!' said the man. 'For, as it happens, I am a cow-tamer. Only I lost my cow last week. She escaped and bit three people's heads off.'

'Goodness!' said Jack.

'So I will need to buy another cow, but she must be extremely fierce.'

As I've already told you, Jack was an honest boy, but hunger had made him desperate.

'Why, Pansy is the fiercest cow there is!' said Jack. 'She used to be a pirate and was the terror of the seven seas. Pansy, show the man how fierce you are!'

Pansy did some poo.

'She *does* seem fierce!' said the funny-looking man. 'I will buy her.'

'And what will you give me for her?' asked Jack.

The man dropped a small bag into Jack's hand. 'Look inside!' he chuckled.

The bag was full of bran.

'No deal!' said Jack. 'You will have to find another ferocious cow, for I am nobody's fool!'

'But it's magic bran!' said the man.

'Oh, well, that's different,' said Jack.

'What did you get for Pansy?' asked the widow when Jack returned.

'You'll never guess!' said Jack.

'A piece of gold?'

'What I have here is better than gold,' said Jack. 'It's bran.'

'I see,' said the widow. She took a deep breath. 'Jack, have you ever heard of something called a gold rush?'

'I have,' said Jack. 'People risk their very lives to travel to distant places and dig in the earth. It is back-breaking toil but sometimes they discover gold and become rich.'

The widow nodded. 'And have you ever heard of something called a bran rush?'

'Do people risk their lives for bran as well?' asked Jack in amazement.

'No, they don't,' said the widow. 'Because bran

is worth about as much as a pat of Pansy's poo.'

'But this is magic bran!' said Jack.

'Magic bran indeed!' said the widow. 'And you, my child, are a total dunce!'

Angrily, the widow threw the bran out the window. 'Now, off to bed with you, foolish boy!'

'Can I have a candle, Mother?' asked Jack.

'No!' snapped the widow. 'I ate them all.'

Jack had an uncomfortable night. His stomach was rumbling most terribly and he kept seeing a horrible vision of his mother at the end of his bed, pointing at him and jeering, although it wasn't really a vision because she was actually doing it.

When Jack got up the next morning he noticed something peculiar outside his window. It was his mother again. But she was pointing at an enormous plant that had grown up during the night. It reached right up to the sky and beyond the clouds.

'I told you it was magic bran!' said Jack. 'It has grown into a magic branstalk!'

'I've never heard such piffle!' said the widow. 'Next you'll be saying it leads to the house of some hideous giant who has a goose that lays golden eggs!'

'Actually, I wasn't going to say that,' said Jack, leaping straight from his bedroom window onto the enormous plant. 'But just you watch me climb it!'

'Not until you put your pants on,' said the widow.

Jack climbed the branstalk for hours and hours until at the very top he did indeed find himself before the front door of a giant's house.

There was a doormat the size of a football field and it had the word UNWELCOME on it.

'Who goes there?'

Jack spun around to see a fierce-looking woman who wasn't much bigger than he was.

'My name is Jack,' he said.

'Are you a human?' the fierce woman asked.

'I am,' said Jack.

'Then flee if you value your life! My husband is a giant who can bend jumbo jets into pretzels.

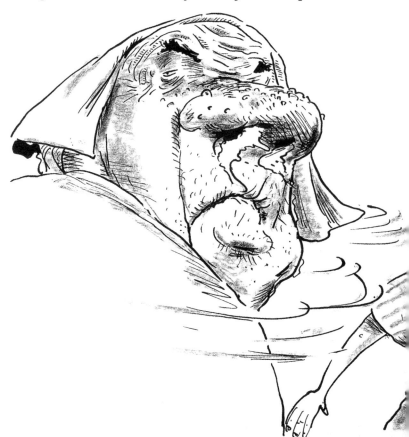

He will kill you and use you as a cotton bud to clean his ears, for he cannot stand humans.'

'Then why hasn't he killed *you*?' asked Jack.

'I'm a giant, you dingbat!'

'You're quite small for a giant.'

'I have a cold,' said the fierce woman. 'And when giants get colds, we shrink.'

'I may be able to help you,' said Jack brightly, 'for I am a vegetarian and we know how to stop contracting colds.'

'Hush!' cried the woman. 'My husband approaches!'

The whole place shook, and Jack heard a blood-curdling voice rip through the air like thunder.

'*Fee-fi-fo-fum!*
I smell the blood of an Englishman!'

(This surprised Jack, because he was actually from Sydney. It also didn't rhyme very well.)

The hideous giant towered over Jack. He had sharp yellow teeth and a terrible red face and problem hair. A huge boot came down and Jack had to move quickly to avoid being trodden on.

'Why are you trying to kill me?' cried Jack. 'I've done you no harm.'

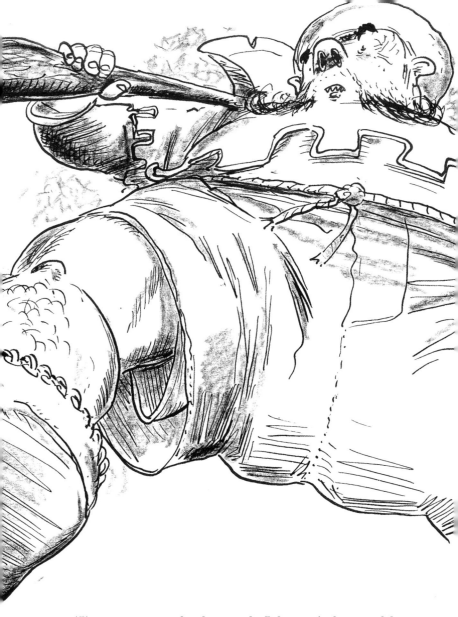

'I'm in a very bad mood. I haven't been able to go to the toilet for fifty years!' shouted the giant, bringing down his other boot.

'Ah, that means you are constipated!' yelled Jack, jumping for his life as the boot crashed down. 'You need a laxative!'

'What is this laxative of which you speak?' asked the giant.

'It will help unblock you!' answered Jack. 'The best laxative in the world is bran. And I happen to know where you can get all the bran you could want!'

Following Jack's advice, the giant hacked off a huge hunk of the branstalk and ate it. Moments later he went running off to his giant lavatory and was there for quite some time. When he returned he had a lovely wide grin on his face.

'Fee-fi-fo-fum!
You'll never guess what I've just done!'

'You've cured my husband, you clever boy!' wheezed the woman. 'Even his rhymes are getting better. Now, what about my cold?'

Jack always kept strange herbs and such things in his pocket. He handed her a mysterious little object.

'What is this sorcery?' she asked.

'It is a magic charm called an inhaler.'

'What do I do with it?'

'Stick it up your nose,' Jack said wisely.

The woman did as he said. Immediately she stopped sneezing and felt much better and grew back to her proper giant size, which was even bigger than her husband.

Now both the giants were happy, and they playfully punched each other on the arm and gave each other loving head-butts.

Bidding farewell to the cheerful giants, Jack slid down the enormous branstalk to tell his mother the wonderful news that they were no longer poor because the giants had given him twenty thousand dollars for curing them.

The old widow was at the bottom of the enormous plant looking very angry indeed and holding up a newspaper. On the front page was a picture of Pansy the cow riding a bicycle on a tightrope. She had just joined a circus in Las Vegas and they were paying her a million dollars a year.

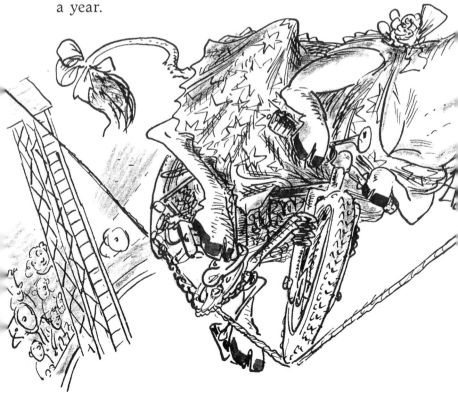

But Jack and his mother did all right. With the giants' money, Jack set up a health food shop that sold nuts and carob and that weird grass stuff. The most popular product was the wonderful bran cake Jack made, so no one suffered constipation ever again and even the widow was happy.

The moral of this story is: You shouldn't count your chickens unless you're bored and can't think of anything better to do.

Cinderolla

Once upon a time there was a lady scientist and a gentleman scientist. They loved each other very much so they decided to get married. Now, some scientists can be attractive, but these two weren't. However, it didn't matter because they had good hearts and bad eyesight.

When their first daughter was born she was seriously ugly, with a face like a prawn pizza. But, unlike her parents, she did not have a good heart. She threw jam jars at all the other children and set fire to her teddy and tied large helium balloons to her grandma so she floated away to China.

This little girl was the most horrible child in the world. She only became the second-most horrible child in the world when her sister was born.

The two ugly sisters grew bigger and uglier, and the scientists decided it might be a mistake to have any more children in case they turned out just as dreadful. And so they decided to build themselves a beautiful little robot girl who had everything the ugly sisters did not, such as a nice personality, a sweet voice and wheels. They called her Cinderolla.

The two scientists introduced Cinderolla to her ugly sisters and told them to look after her.

'We'll look after her all right,' said the ugly sisters, sticking fridge magnets to her.

One afternoon they took her to the park.

'I am having such a lovely day,' said Cinderolla, gliding around on her little wheels and looking at all the smiling children walking their puppy dogs. 'Was ever a girl so happy?'

'Shut up!' said the ugly sisters.

'What does *shut up* mean?' asked Cinderolla.

'It is a polite way of saying hello to police officers,' said the ugly sisters.

Cinderolla happily said 'Shut up!' to three police officers. She was immediately put in gaol and the scientists had to bail her out.

'What did I do wrong?' Cinderolla asked her ugly sisters.

'You should only say *Shut up!* to a policeman when he is on a horse.'

'Oh, I see. How do I say hello to a normal policeman?'

'*Up yours!*' said the ugly sisters.

The next day Cinderolla met the same three police officers and ended up in gaol again.

The ugly sisters got nastier and nastier. One day they took Cinderolla shopping. She saw a little boy riding on a mechanical elephant and said she would like a ride like that. So the ugly sisters took her to a paint shop. They paid the shopkeeper to let Cinderolla sit on the paint-mixing machine and then they switched it on.

Cinderolla was shaken about so much that it scrambled her hard drive and for days she could only talk rap.

Years later, the scientists passed away. The ugly sisters were now adults who still lived in their parents' house. They kept Cinderolla as their slave to help them into their corsets and pull the hairs out of their ears.

One day a carrier pigeon arrived at the house. It was carrying a royal invitation, along with a bunch of junk mail advertising an all-night supermarket. The invitation was from a handsome Prince who was throwing a royal ball.

The ugly sisters were very excited. They raced out to buy the finest ball gowns that the all-night supermarket had to offer.

'I would so like to go to the Prince's ball,' said Cinderolla, longingly.

'The very idea!' scoffed the ugly sisters. 'A royal ball is no place for *robots*!'

The sisters rode off to the palace in a turbo-charged chariot, leaving Cinderolla all alone to scrub the floors.

As Cinderolla toiled away, some pink smoke filled the air, and before her there appeared a beautiful fairy with a wand and a suitcase.

'Who are you?' gasped Cinderolla.

'I am your fairy godmother,' said the

beautiful fairy. 'I also sell cosmetics because there isn't much money in being a fairy godmother.'

Cinderolla was so surprised that her jaw dropped. She picked it up and stuck it on again.

'Would you like to go to the Prince's ball?' asked the fairy godmother.

'With all my heart!' said Cinderolla.

'And would you like to try this new shade of lipstick that is on special this week?' asked the fairy godmother, opening her suitcase full of cosmetics.

'No,' said Cinderolla.

The godmother looked disappointed, but waved her magic wand over a pumpkin she had placed on the floor. It turned into a superb coach covered in gold.

'Here is your coach to take you to the ball!' said the fairy godmother.

'Cool!' said Cinderolla.

'Now, do you have six mice?' asked the fairy godmother.

'Why, are you hungry?' asked Cinderolla.

'I do not wish to eat the mice, foolish child. I will turn them into horses to pull your golden coach.'

And that is precisely what the fairy godmother did.

'Now, if you find me six lizards from the garden, I will turn them into six footmen,' she said.

'We don't need six footmen,' said Cinderolla. 'The kitchen is already full of horses and a coach, and frankly it's getting a bit crowded. One of the horses has done something nasty and I'm the one who'll have to clean it up. So can we please get this magic bit over and done with?'

'Very well,' said the fairy godmother. 'You cannot go to the ball wearing those stinking rags or people will think you're a children's book illustrator.'

She waved her wand and Cinderolla was dressed in a magnificent gown that reached to the floor and hid her wheels.

'Now,' said the fairy godmother hopefully, 'would you like to try this face cream for a younger, fresher look?'

'No,' said Cinderolla. 'I am off to the ball!'

'Enjoy yourself, Cinderolla! But be sure to leave before the clock strikes midnight. For then the magic spell will wear off and your coach will turn back into a pumpkin and your clothes will become just as they were before.'

'It's not much of a magic spell if it only lasts for a few hours,' said Cinderolla.

'That's your fault for not buying any cosmetics,' said the fairy godmother, and she vanished in a big pink huff.

Cinderolla had the most marvellous time at the ball. The Prince was enchanted by the mystery guest. 'Who is this girl who looks like an angel and moves like a skateboard?' he wondered.

Cinderolla was overjoyed when he asked her to dance.

'You are the most beautiful girl I have ever seen,' the Prince told her.

'So are you,' said Cinderolla.

'I would like to dance with you all night.'

'I can only dance till midnight,' said Cinderolla.

'Why is that?'

'Because then my dress will come off.'

'Oh!' said the Prince, who had fallen in love.

The ugly sisters jealously watched the Prince dance with the beautiful girl and had no idea she was Cinderolla. They were stupid as well as ugly. The hours flew past, and before Cinderolla knew it the clock in the palace tower struck midnight.

'Beep!' it chimed, twelve times. It was a fairly modern clock.

Cinderolla rolled away from the ball as quickly as she could.

'Goodbye, my love!' cried the Prince.

'Knicker elastic, my love!' cried Cinderolla, because her wicked sisters had told her this was how you said farewell to a member of the royal family.

Cinderolla raced down the palace stairs, but as she did so one of her wheels fell off. She disappeared into the night and the Prince picked up the wheel. 'I will search every house in the land until I find the owner of this wheel,' vowed the Prince, 'for she shall be my babe.'

When it became known that the Prince was looking for someone who rolled about, many ladies attached skateboard wheels to their feet, and there was a great deal of grinding throughout the land.

The ugly sisters were determined to marry the Prince and had themselves fitted with brand new skateboard wheels. Of course, the sisters didn't realise that the mysterious girl the Prince sought was their own robot sister Cinderolla.

One morning the Prince and his royal attendants came to the house where the ugly sisters lived. They tried to fit the wheel to each of the sisters, without success.

'Does someone else live in this house?' the Prince asked.

'Only Cinderolla,' snapped the older ugly sister. 'She's on the roof. We've been using her as a TV antenna.'

The royal attendants fetched Cinderolla down. When the Prince placed the wheel on her foot, he found it fitted perfectly.

So Cinderolla and the Prince had a big royal wedding, and one year later Cinderolla gave birth to a beautiful baby toaster. And the fairy godmother sold all her cosmetics to the ugly sisters so they weren't ugly any more, and everyone lived happily ever after.

The moral of this story is: A watched pot never boils, but an egg in the microwave always explodes.

Puss in Blots

Once upon a time there was a miller who died and left his estate to his three sons. The eldest got one half of the mill, the second got the other half, and the youngest, whose name was Clint, got nothing but the cat. Clint was annoyed because *he* was the one who did most of the work in the mill, while his brothers spent all their time playing video games.

'My brothers,' said Clint, 'won't you share the mill with me? All I have is this dumb cat. I will be unemployed and out in the cold.'

'Begone with you!' said the selfish brothers. 'And if the cold bothers you, why don't you make a muff out of the cat?'

Now, the cat certainly didn't want to be made

into a muff. He didn't like the idea of someone sticking their hands up both his ends. But he was afraid this would happen unless he thought of something fast. And so he decided to speak to Clint.

'It is quite warm today,' said the cat, as he walked alongside Clint. 'There is certainly no need to wear fur of any sort.'

'It is snowing, you idiot,' said Clint. Then he realised the cat had spoken and was most amazed.

'Have you always been able to talk?' he asked.

The cat nodded. 'I used to belong to a witch. She couldn't afford a broom so she flew around on a toilet-brush.'

'How dreadful!' said Clint with a shudder.

'You can see why I escaped.'

'That's very interesting,' said Clint, 'but it doesn't help me because I have no money and I'm freezing cold.'

'Don't worry,' said the cat. 'I will get a bag of gold from the King.'

'Are you sure you can do that?' asked Clint in wonder.

'When you've flown around the world balancing on the bristles of a toilet-brush, you can do anything,' said the cat.

Now, neither the cat nor Clint had been reading the newspapers lately, or they would have known that the King was a miserable old coot. He wanted everyone else to be miserable as well. If anyone smiled or laughed they were locked in prison or chucked in the sea. Squads of Misery Police went around cutting yo-yo strings and popping balloons and removing the jokes from bonbons, even the 'knock-knock' ones, which were usually bad. The TV stations never showed comedies, only nasty shows like *Celebrity Houses on Fire* or *Explode Your Granny* or *See What Happens When a Fridge Drops on You.*

The unwary cat and Clint arrived at the castle. On the way the cat had picked a bag of mushrooms so he had a present to give the King.

'You wait here and I will return with a bag of gold, just you see!' said the cat.

The cat left and Clint started whistling a happy tune until the Misery Police came and told him to shut up or they would stick a cork in his gob and chuck him in the sea.

The King was in his throne room, writing his birthday speech. Every year when it was his birthday he went on television to tell the people about his troubles and his itchy feet and the dreadful pimple on the back of his neck. He was just writing the part about how much he hated mushrooms when the cat jumped up on his desk.

'Greetings!' the cat said. 'I come with a gift from my master!' And he placed the bag on the desk.

'I hope those aren't mushrooms,' said the King. 'For it is known throughout the land that I hate mushrooms.'

'Er, they're strawberries,' said the cat. 'Even if they do look a bit mushroomy.'

'Poppycock!' yelled the King. He brought his fist down to whack the cat, but the nimble creature leaped out of the way, knocking over the King's bottle of black ink as he did so.

The King was furious. He was about to order that the cat be chucked in the sea, when he noticed that the blot had formed an interesting shape on the parchment.

'It reminds me of my mother,' he said, frowning.

'Really?' said the cat, sensing he might be able to avoid a soggy fate if he kept the King talking. 'Did you *like* your mother?'

'I did not,' said the King. 'It's her fault I started smoking.'

'Why is it her fault?' asked the cat.

'She set fire to me,' replied the King.

'I see,' said the cat, making another blot. 'And what do you see here, Your Majesty?'

'It looks like my father.'

'It's a very small and ugly blot,' said the cat.

'He was a very small and ugly father,' said the King, bursting into tears.

'Well!' said the cat. 'It is your parents who have made you so unhappy. You must hug them and forgive them! Then you should find a wife! And you mustn't chuck her in the sea, because wives don't like that.'

The King was impressed by the cat's advice. He hugged his parents, even though they were dead. Then he found a wife on the Internet and they were married the very next day. And people were allowed to laugh again, even at the stupid jokes that had mysteriously started appearing in fairytales. In gratitude, the King gave the cat a bag of gold.

Clint was happy to see the cat again, and even happier when he saw the bag of gold.

'How did you get it?' asked Clint.

'I got the King to look at an inkblot and he saw all sorts of strange things,' said the cat. 'Then he told me about the strange things and paid me some money.'

'But that's silly!' said Clint.

'No, I prefer to call it *psychiatry*,' said the cat. 'And I think it's going to make us both a lot of money.'

Word spread throughout the land about the clever cat who could solve all your problems by getting you to look at inkblots and talk your head off. With the money they made, the cat and Clint bought a fine office in the heart of the city. Clint wasn't clever enough to do the trick with the inkblots, so he became the cat's receptionist. It was his job to collect the money from the patients and answer the phones and send naughty jokes by e-mail all day long.

One day a beautiful girl with blonde hair and blue eyes came to visit the cat. When Clint saw her in the waiting room reading an old issue of *Witches' Weekly*, he immediately fell in love with her. He secretly told the cat that whatever the girl saw in the inkblot, the cat must tell her she should marry Clint the receptionist.

'What does this remind you of?' asked the cat, showing an inkblot to the girl, whose name was Mary Mary.

'That looks like my garden,' said Mary Mary.

The cat didn't think it looked like a garden at all.

'What exactly do you have in your garden?' he asked.

'Silver bells and cockleshells,' said Mary Mary.

'How unusual!' said the cat, looking puzzled. 'Anything else?'

'Pretty maids all in a row,' said Mary Mary.

'Excuse me a moment,' said the cat, leaving his office.

'You cannot marry her,' he said to Clint. 'She's bonkers.'

'How do you know?' asked Clint.

'She says her garden is full of pretty maids. I think she must have buried them there.'

The cat returned to his office. Clint was sad to learn that the beautiful girl was bonkers. But when Mary Mary emerged from the office, Clint was again struck by her loveliness and knelt down before her.

'Oh Mary Mary, is it true that your garden is full of dead bodies?' he asked.

'It most certainly is not!' snapped Mary Mary.

'Then what are these pretty maids all in a row?' asked Clint.

Mary sighed. 'Foolish boy! My pretty maids are all statues. Have you never heard of statues before?'

Clint shook his head. 'I am a simple miller's son.'

'Well, statues are people carved of stone, and usually they have no clothes on,' said Mary Mary.

'Oh,' said Clint. 'Will you please take me to see your garden?'

'I'm afraid I can't,' said Mary Mary. 'The cat wants to send me to a mysterious place he calls a funny farm.'

'Don't worry,' said Clint. 'I'll have a word with him about that. Are you sure these statues have no clothes on?'

'Not a stitch,' said Mary Mary.

'I'll be right back,' said Clint.

Clint explained everything to the cat, who decided that Mary Mary wasn't bonkers after all, just a bit contrary.

And when Mary Mary showed Clint her garden and he smiled so pleasantly, she thought what a fine young man he was, even if he did spend a bit too much time looking at the statues. So when Clint asked Mary Mary to be his bride, she said yes.

They were married right there in the garden with the cat as the best man. Mary Mary's sister Lucy Lucy was the bridesmaid. The guests were Tom Tom the piper's son, Dan Dan the lavatory man and Twinkle Twinkle the little star. They danced the can-can and the cha-cha, and then everyone rode home on a choo-choo.

The moral of this story is: An apple a day keeps the doctor away. Particularly if you aim for the head.

Little Reg Riding Hood

Once upon a time there was a handsome boy called Little Reg Riding Hood. He was so named because he was very proud of his jacket. It had a hood and it was made of velvet and lined with silk. (Silk may seem very grand, but it is made from the stuff silkworms throw up. So when you lie in a bed with silk sheets you are actually lying in something that used to be worm sick.)

Reg had made the jacket himself and he wore it everywhere, even when he was forced to play football with other boys. They poked fun at him, but Reg didn't care.

'You are just jealous because I look so fine in my velvet jacket,' said Reg, 'and my bright green pantaloons and silver gloves with frills on.'

The boys never kicked the ball to him.

Reg's widowed father worked at an iron foundry that made suits of armour for fat knights. It was back-breaking toil, especially when the knights returned for alterations, and Reg's father was always in a terrible mood when he came home.

'What is that gaudy scarf tied around your head, boy?' Reg's father asked gruffly, eating the pastries his son had made for his tea.

'It is called a bandanna,' said Reg.

'Bunk!' growled his father, which is an old-fashioned word meaning *hogwash*. 'A bandanna is a long yellow fruit that monkeys eat.'

'You are thinking of a banana,' said Reg. 'If a monkey ate a bandanna it would be sick.'

'Double bunk!' growled his father, which is an old-fashioned word meaning *one bed on top of another*. 'Don't be clever to your father! Take that and that and that!'

Fortunately, Reg's father never actually hit him. All he did was sit there saying, 'Take that and that and that!' But Reg still didn't like it.

One day Reg's father came home from the iron foundry with the news that he had been sacked because of the bad state of the economy and also because the other workers there hated his guts. Reg's father couldn't find any other work and soon there was no money for pastries and they began to starve.

'You will have to go to visit your grandmother,' said Reg's father. 'She will give us money, for she is my own dear mother and I love her with all my heart, even though I forget where she lives.'

'I remember,' said Reg. 'Her house is next to that shop where I bought the pink shell buttons for those overalls I made you.'

'Do not speak of those wretched frilly overalls!' said his father. 'When the foreman saw me he laughed so hard he fell into a vat of molten steel and now he is a set of saucepans.'

Little Reg Riding Hood skipped merrily through the deep dark woods on his way to Grandma's place.

It so happened that a wolf lived in these woods, and he was stroppy because his dear wife and twin children had been killed by hunters.

His wife had been made into a fur coat and the twins had been made into a fur bikini. When Little Reg Riding Hood came skipping along the path, the wolf decided he would eat him up in revenge. However, the clever wolf knew that if he ate up Reg right away, the boy would probably make a bit of a noise, as people usually do when you eat them up because they are such sooks. And the noise might attract the hunters nearby. So the wolf pretended he was friendly and asked Reg where he was going.

'I am off to Grandma's house to scrounge some money from her,' said Reg.

'Where does your grandma live?' asked the wolf, a plan forming in his big hairy head.

'On the other side of the deep dark woods,' said Reg. 'Next to the button shop.'

'I will race you there!' said the wolf.

'I don't like racing or sports in general,' said Reg.

'I didn't think so,' said the wolf.

And Reg skipped off.

Now, the wolf knew the deep dark woods like the back of his paw. He took a short cut to the old lady's house and knocked at the door: *Tap, tap.*

'Who's there?' a frail old voice asked.

'Batman!' replied the wolf, cunningly.

The grandmother was delighted to think that such a famous person should come to visit her. But when she opened her door, hoping to see a dashing superhero, she was shocked to see a huge beast with saliva dripping from his teeth.

The wolf swallowed the grandmother whole and then went upstairs to try on her dresses, which is something the real Batman would *never* do. He much prefers tights and undies.

Some time afterwards Little Reg Riding Hood knocked at the door: *Tap, tap.*

'Who's there?' asked the wolf, imitating an old lady.

'It is Little Reg Riding Hood. What is wrong with your voice?'

'I have been smoking Cuban cigars,' said the wolf.

Little Reg Riding Hood was suspicious because his grandmother never smoked Cuban cigars, only Indian ones, but he entered her house all the same.

Upstairs was the wolf, dressed in ladies' clothes and lying in the grandmother's bed.

'It is good to see you again, Little Reg Riding

Hood,' said the wolf. 'Come closer so I may gaze upon your handsome face!'

'But Grandma, what big ears you have!' said Reg.

'All the better to hear you with,' said the wolf.

'But Grandma, what big arms you have!' said Reg.

'All the better to hug you with,' said the wolf.

'But Grandma, what big boobs you have!' said Reg.

'Now you're just being rude,' said the wolf.

'No, you look very nice in that peasant blouse,' said Reg. 'But the necklace is a bit much.'

'Could you please remove it for me, dear Reg,' said the wolf, 'since I am so old and frail?'

When Reg tried to remove the necklace, the wolf snarled fiercely.

'You're not my grandmother!' Reg cried in alarm.

'I swallowed her!' laughed the terrible wolf.
'And now I will swallow you too!'

The wolf jumped up and pounced on Reg.

'Don't eat me!' said Reg. 'You'll get fat.'

'Oh dear, you're right,' said the wolf.

'I have a better idea,' said Reg. 'With your sense of style we could go into business together making fake furs, and no one would ever need to skin a wolf again.'

'What a good idea!' said the wolf.

'But first you will have to throw up my grandmother, for she is a sweet old lady even if she stinks of cigars.'

'And how will I do that?' asked the wolf.

'Eat my bandanna. For it is widely known that bandannas make animals sick.'

'Is it?'

'If you'd been paying attention you'd have heard me say it at the start of the story.'

So the wolf swallowed Reg's bandanna and moments later he threw up the grandmother.

'*Batman* my backside!' cried the old lady.

Well, the two business partners made a fortune together in the fashion industry. The wolf became a supermodel and he was so handsome that when he walked by everyone whistled at him. And that is where we get the word *wolf-whistle* from, although why we say *catwalk* is anyone's guess.

Reg's father started wearing the clothes that Reg designed, including pirate pants and puffy shirts. He even wore a big bandanna around his head, although he couldn't tie it properly and it kept falling down over his eyes. 'I taught my son Reg everything he knows!' he boasted to a television crew one day. Then he walked off into a wall.

The moral of this story is: A bird in the hand is bound to poo on you eventually, so let it go.

The Princess and the Peg

Once upon a time there was a handsome but lonely Prince who dearly wanted to marry a Princess. Sadly, there was a national Princess shortage because so many of them had been eaten by dragons. Others had decided to become children's authors and had died of starvation. The Prince was about to give up hope. He decided that if he couldn't meet a Princess he would have to marry a commoner instead. There is nothing wrong with being a commoner, but the Prince was a bit of a snob. He wanted to marry someone who knew about horseriding and hunting and skiing and opening hospitals and all the things Princesses are supposed to know about.

Impostors in cardboard crowns kept coming to the castle, pretending they were Princesses so they could marry the Prince and be rich. Usually the King was wise enough to spot that they were not Princesses at all, especially the men.

But a rather clever young girl had done her homework, and one evening she knocked at the door of the castle.

'Who ventures out on such a terrible night?' the King asked when he saw the drenched girl at his door.

'My name is Tamsin,' said the girl.

'Why are you drenched?' the King asked, for it was not raining.

'I fell in your stupid moat,' said Tamsin.

'Oh dear, that would explain the duck on your head,' said the King. 'Unless you normally wear a duck when you go out visiting?'

'No, I do not!' replied Tamsin angrily. 'I normally wear a crown.'

'Then you'd better come in and get out of your wet clothes,' said the King.

'Do you have some dry ones for me to wear?' asked Tamsin.

'No,' said the King. 'You'll just have to dance around in your undies till you're dry.'

'I will come in but I will not dance around in my undies, for I am a Princess!' said Tamsin.

'You're the third one today,' sighed the King. But he invited her in anyway. He made the duck stay outside.

The King led Tamsin into the parlour.

'Do you wish to marry my son?' he asked.

'I do,' said Tamsin, 'for he is a spunkrat.'

'Then you must dine with us tonight!' said the King.

'What are you having?'

'Fish and chips.'

'Princesses don't eat fish and chips!' scoffed Tamsin.

This was true. Could the girl be a Princess after all? Thoughtfully, the King stroked his beard. 'What *would* you like for dinner, Princess Tamsin?'

'A stuffed quail,' said Tamsin.

'What would you like it stuffed with?' asked the King.

'A giraffe,' said Tamsin.

This was a very royal thing to eat, and the King felt encouraged.

'You're in luck,' he smiled. 'We have a giraffe in the freezer. Although I might have to send in to town for the quail.'

That night the King and the Prince and Tamsin sat down to a feast of quail stuffed with giraffe. Unfortunately the Queen could not join them because she was dead. The King had shot her while hunting for bears. He said it was an accident. It was true the Queen *did* look a bit like a bear, but people were still suspicious, especially when the King did cartwheels at her funeral.

The King was still trying to work out if Tamsin was a real Princess or not.

'Do you go skiing, Princess Tamsin?' he asked.

'Oh yes,' said Tamsin. 'I just got back from Switzerland.'

'And how did you find it?' asked the King.

'With an atlas,' said Tamsin.

'That's not a proper answer!' snapped the King. 'You're an impostor!'

'It was a joke, noodle-brain!' said Tamsin.

The King was delighted. Only a Princess would be bold enough to call the King a noodle-brain.

'Do you enjoy opening hospitals?' he asked.

'I *adore* opening hospitals,' replied Tamsin. 'Often I make them close just so I can open them again.'

This all seemed very promising.

'And I expect you must enjoy hunting as well?' said the King.

'But of course!' cried Tamsin. 'I learned hunting when I went to Princess School.'

'And what did you hunt for?' asked the King.

'Teachers, mainly,' replied Tamsin sweetly.

'That must have led to staff shortages,' said the King.

'It did,' nodded Tamsin, 'which is why I can't add up or spell or do anything except hunt and ski and open hospitals.'

The King smiled. Their visitor certainly seemed like a real Princess.

The Prince was starting to fall in love with Tamsin, so he decided to make small talk with her. (Small talk means *chatting*, which you have to do if you are royal. It doesn't mean talking about small things, such as germs. A true royal person would never start a conversation by saying, 'Hello, you seem to have a lot of germs.')

'Something rather interesting happened to a friend of mine,' said the Prince, talking his best small talk. 'A witch turned him into a frog! It was very embarrassing. French people kept trying to eat his legs.'

'How fascinating!' said Tamsin. 'A witch turned my father into a pig! It took us a year before we realised.'

'You have to be careful of witches,' said the Prince.

'It's one of the problems of being royal,' agreed Tamsin.

There was now hardly a doubt in the King's mind that their visitor was genuine royalty. 'Will you stay the night, Princess Tamsin?' he asked.

'No,' said Tamsin. 'I have to get up early tomorrow morning to open six hospitals.'

'Pretty please?' begged the Prince.

'What's for breakfast?' asked Tamsin.

'Sausages,' said the King.

'Princesses don't eat sausages,' sneered Tamsin.

'They are made from endangered species,' said the King grandly.

'Then I will stay,' said Tamsin.

Tamsin finished her royal hot chocolate and padded off to one of the twenty-three bathrooms to prepare for bed.

The King told the Prince he had one final test to work out if Tamsin was a real Princess or not. In one of the guest bedrooms he pulled all the bedclothes off the bed. He put a tiny pea on the bedstead. Then he covered it with twenty mattresses, one upon another. He explained to the Prince, 'If she is a true Princess she will not sleep a wink tonight because she will feel the hard little pea under all the mattresses and it will be an unbearable lump in the bed. But if she is a mere commoner she will feel nothing and sleep like a log.'

'You're a boob,' said the Prince. 'You've used a cooked pea.'

'Botheration!' said the King.

He pulled away the twenty mattresses. Then he scraped the badly squashed pea off the bedstead and tried to find a hard uncooked one to replace it with. But there were no hard peas in the entire castle, so he took a clothes peg from the laundry and used that instead.

'This will work just as well,' said the King.

'You're making this up as you go along,' said the Prince.

'Shut up!' said the King.

The King and the Prince wished Tamsin goodnight, and when they had gone she chuckled to think how she had fooled them both. For Tamsin wasn't a Princess at all, she was just a girl who worked in a dress shop putting those little dye-bombs on posh frocks to prevent shoplifting. Only she got sacked because she was so bored one day that she chucked a dozen of the dye-bombs into a rude rich lady's pram. They all went off when the lady left the store and her baby was bright green for a week.

Tamsin climbed up the ridiculously high tower of mattresses and fell asleep. She dreamed of marrying the handsome Prince. She also had one of those peculiar dreams where you are desperate to go to the toilet and you manage to find one, only of course it isn't a real toilet. But you don't work that out until it's too late.

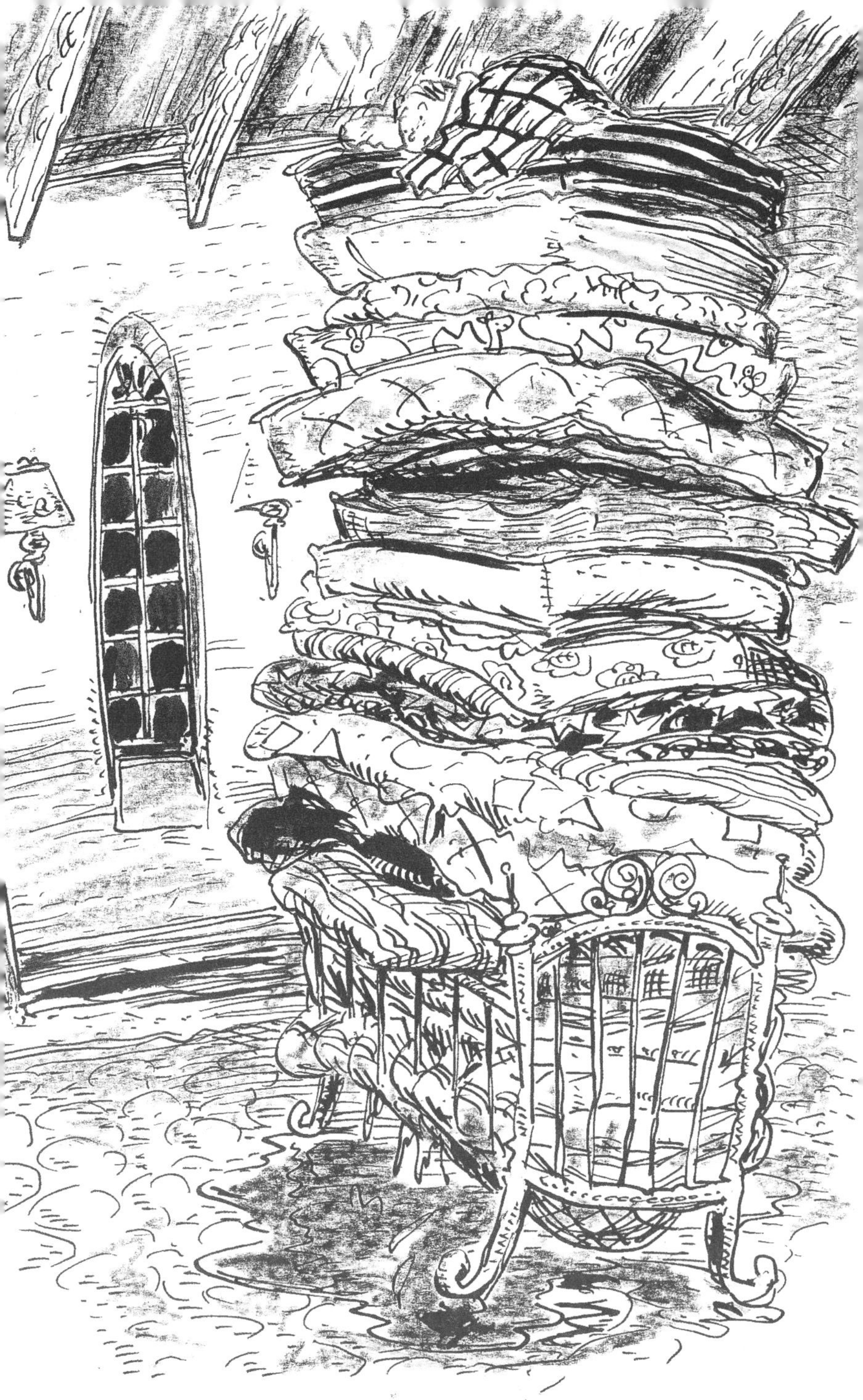

The next morning, as they ate their panda sausages, the King asked Tamsin how she had slept.

'Very badly indeed!' said Tamsin.

'Oh, what wonderful news!' cried the Prince. 'For that means you must be a real Princess after all and we shall get married!'

Tamsin was happy to go along with this plan. Anything was better than selling dresses to annoying rich ladies.

The King was delighted and ran off to organise the wedding. He didn't realise that Tamsin had slept badly because she had wet the bed after drinking so much hot chocolate and it had nothing to do with the clothes peg at all.

But it really didn't matter because Tamsin and the Prince made a nice married couple. When Tamsin found out about the peg under all the mattresses she pretended that this was of course the reason she couldn't sleep. (Tamsin's family motto was *Fibbius incendium pantaloonium*, which translates as *Liar, liar, pants on fire*.)

Soon everyone throughout the land knew the story of the Princess and the peg. Whenever Tamsin passed, people put pegs on their noses as a sign of respect.

The poet laureate even made up a special poem:

God save Princess Tamsin,
Dressed in panda fur!
When we see a clothes peg,
We will think of her.
As we do our washing
And we hang it high,
We will think of Tamsin
While our knickers dry.

The poet laureate lost his job shortly afterwards. But the Prince and Tamsin both lived happily ever after, except when Tamsin drank too much hot chocolate before bed.

The moral of this story is: People of different races and colours can live together happily. Tamsin and the Prince were actually of the same race and colour, but it's still a good moral.

(Please note that no animals were harmed in this fairytale. All that stuff about eating endangered species was utter rubbish. No teachers were harmed either. And the duck ended up as Prime Minister.)

What happened next

The Honeybump Publishing Company published more books than any other company in the universe. *Baby's First Robbery*, *Let's Cook a Hat* and *The Toilet Pixies* were just three of their famous titles.

Leon Stumble was nervous as he sat with Cassie in the foyer of the huge building waiting to see the children's book publisher, Una Spooner. Under his arm he held a folder that contained the five fairytales he had written so far.

'These stories are a bit stupid, Cassie,' said Leon. 'In fact, I don't think I've ever written anything quite so stupid before.'

'Relax, Leon,' said Cassie, who sat at his side. 'We'll wait to see what Una Spooner has to say.'

'I wish I had a cup of coffee,' said Leon.

A paper cup of coffee appeared in his hand and he sipped. Cassie's little act of magic didn't strike Leon as odd because he was too nervous about seeing the publisher. He was as unobservant as ever.

'Hello, I'm Una Spooner,' said a handsome woman in expensive Italian clothes. 'You must be Leon Stumble. I'm ready to see you now. You have precisely three-and-a-half minutes.'

Una Spooner's luxurious office was closed off from the rest of the building. She didn't want to be interrupted by people gazing at her through the glass, begging not to be sacked. The office was full of all the awards that Una's books had won. The biggest of all was a golden one that had pride of place on the trophy shelf. The engraving on the base said it was a Lifetime Achievement Award for Una's contribution to children's literature. The metal thing on top was in the shape of a human bottom.

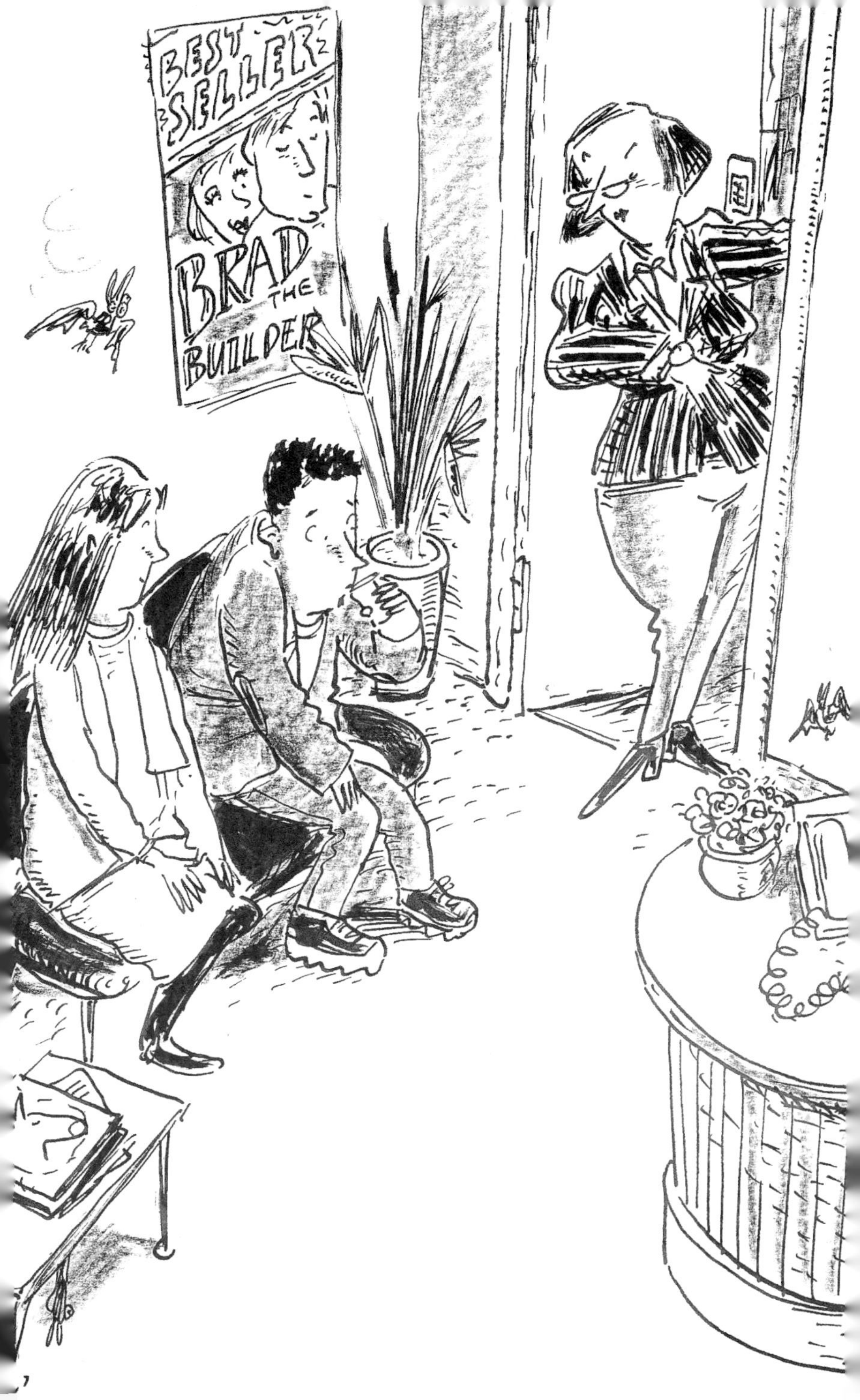
BEST SELLER
BRAD THE BUILDER

Una looked thoughtful. 'Leon Stumble. Where have I heard that name before?'

'It's a fairly common name,' said Leon.

'You're not the Leon Stumble who's been sending me all those awful books about coal and paste?' asked Una.

'No, and not about turkeys either,' said Leon.

'I'm glad to hear it,' said Una. 'So what have *you* got for me?'

'Fairytales,' said Leon.

Una rolled her eyes.

'With unusual titles,' added Cassie.

Una rolled her eyes back in the other direction.

'I'm sorry about this,' said Leon. He was starting to feel flustered. 'I think we should probably go. Come on, Cassie.'

But Cassie wasn't going anywhere just yet. There were three phones on Una's desk. The middle one rang. (It was the only one that actually worked. The other two were there to make Una look more important.) Una pressed the speaker button.

'What is it, Lisa?' asked Una.

'This is a bit strange,' said Lisa's voice on the speaker. 'Do you think you could pick up the receiver?'

'You don't have to worry about these people here,' said Una. 'They're just about to leave.'

'Well, that's the problem,' said Lisa. 'They can't.'

'Why not?' snapped Una.

'Your office door is jammed,' said Lisa. 'You know that little tiny African violet plant on my desk?'

Una nodded. 'I've never liked it.'

'I wouldn't say that too loudly if I were you,' said Lisa. 'It might hear you.'

'What on earth are you talking about, you peculiar girl?' asked Una.

'It's grown a bit. Well, quite a lot actually. In fact,

it's sprouted vines all over the outer wall of your office.'

Leon looked questioningly at Cassie.

Una paced over to the door and gave it a nudge. It opened just a fraction and the air was filled with a flowery smell.

'I've called for the fire brigade,' said Lisa, as Una returned to her desk.

'What good will that do?' asked Una. 'Don't they normally put out fires?'

'They rescued my cat out of a tree once,' said Lisa. 'Mind you, I had to set the tree on fire before they agreed to come.'

'Very good. Thank you, Lisa.'

Una settled back into her chair and gently tapped her fingertips together.

'Strange business about that giant African violet trapping us in your office like this,' said Cassie.

Una narrowed her eyes as she looked Cassie up and down. 'Excuse me for asking, but are you a writer too?'

'No, I'm a wi ...' Cassie stopped herself just in time. 'A window cleaner. I'm a window cleaner.'

'I thought you were an aerobics teacher!' said Leon.

'But since we're all stuck here together, why don't you look at my boyfriend's fairytales?' suggested Cassie.

'Very well,' said Una. 'But only if you clean my window.'

Una read the fairytales while Leon and Cassie both cleaned the window. Neither Una nor Leon realised it, but Cassie was cleaning the window with a spell which meant that anyone looking into it from outside would see Una in her underwear. Cassie wasn't terribly keen on Una.

'These are stupid,' Una said, when she was done reading the fairytales.

'Yes, they are,' said Leon. 'Sorry to have bothered you.'

'But stupid books are quite popular at the moment,' said Una.

Leon looked hopeful. 'So do you think you might publish my book?'

Una stroked her big metal backside. Absentmindedly she had wandered over to her trophy shelf.

'I'll need to see some more of your work before I make a decision,' said Una. 'Come back when you've written more fairytales. But I'm warning you, they'd better be very stupid. I have the reputation of the Honeybump Publishing Company to consider. I can't risk publishing a book that isn't stupid. I'll look ridiculous.'

A young woman dashed into the office, waving her arms excitedly.

'Who are you?' asked Una.

'I'm Lisa,' the young woman said. 'I've been your personal assistant for five years.'

'Sorry, I didn't recognise you,' Una said. 'What on *earth* are you doing in my office?'

'I've got some good news, Una!' Lisa cried. 'My African violet has shrunk back to normal.'

Leon shot a puzzled look at Cassie, who stared innocently at the ceiling.

'Well, please apologise to those firemen for wasting their time,' said Una.

'Oh they don't mind,' said Lisa. 'As a matter of fact they don't want to go back to the station.'

The firemen had parked their truck outside the

building and extended the ladder so that it reached right up to Una's window. For some reason there were six firemen on top of the ladder, gazing in and laughing their heads off.

Out in the street, Cassie hugged Leon. It was like a scene from a soppy movie only without the pop music.

'Well done, Leon!' Cassie said.

'It was your idea,' said Leon. 'I'm still not quite sure why you were so keen for me to do it in the first place.'

'Don't you feel any ... different?' asked Cassie.

'How do you mean?'

'After writing about giants and talking cats and so forth, don't you have a slightly different view of the world?'

'I do!' said Leon, with amazement in his voice.

Cassie was delighted, until she realised that Leon was looking up and over her shoulder. He was gazing through the window of Una Spooner's office.

'Good heavens!' said Leon. 'Children's publishers are quite peculiar people, aren't they?'

Leon and Cassie went home, and Leon began writing the amazing story of *The Sappy Prince*. Years ago a famous writer called Oscar Wilde had written a beautiful fairytale called *The Happy Prince*. Leon's version was much stupider.

The Sappy Prince

Once upon a time there was a sad old King. He had an only son called Horace who was a nice boy but a bit *sappy*, which is an old-fashioned word meaning *thick*. All Horace did was play his guitar and sing stupid songs like this:

*'Jack be nimble, Jack be quick,
Jack jump over the candlestick.
Jack be clumsy, Jack be slow,
Up in flames his undies go.'*

Horace was a great disappointment to his father, who was bitter because his poor wife the Queen had been eaten by a dragon. The King was haunted by the Queen's final words. They were *'Owww'* and *'Arrghhh'*. The King promised he would richly reward anyone who could bring the dragon's head to the castle.

'Father, I have made a great discovery,' said Horace to the King one morning.

'What is it?' the King asked, expecting a stupid answer.

'If you press your belly-button in really hard it makes you wet yourself.'

'Nincompoop!' snapped the King. 'You must not waste your time on such things. You must learn to be a King!'

'Why?' asked Horace.

'Because one day I will be gone and the job will be yours.'

Horace looked puzzled. 'Where will you be gone?'

'Where do you think?'

'To the shops?'

'I will be *dead*, you sappy boy! And you will have to be King!'

'But I don't want to be King!' said Horace.

The King went bright red. 'In that case, you are no longer my son!'

'You mean I'm your daughter?'

'I mean you must leave this castle and never return until you have done something to make your father proud.'

Horace thought for a moment. 'Would it make you proud if I stuck my finger in my bellybutton?'

'No, it would not!' yelled the King.

And so Prince Horace put his most treasured belongings into a sheet and tied it with rope to the end of a stick. Then he left the castle, carrying the stick over his shoulder and his guitar around his neck. The Prince actually owned a fine suitcase and it would probably have been more sensible to put his belongings in that, but he really was an oafish boy. As he strolled along the road away from the castle he sang another song:

*'See my sweetheart full of grace,
In the grass she settles,
Then she rockets into space,
Propelled by stinging nettles.'*

As he crossed a bridge, the Prince heard a desperate cry coming from the stream below.

'Help! Somebody save me!'

The Prince looked down and saw a tiny man struggling to keep his head above water. He was no bigger than a beansprout.

'What manner of man are you?' asked Horace.

'I am a pixie,' replied the man.

'How do you do?' said Horace. 'I am a nincompoop!'

'I will grant you whatever you want,' spluttered the pixie, 'if you rescue me from this torrent.'

'But how will I rescue you?'

'Throw me a rope!'

The Prince untied the rope from his package of belongings and tossed it into the stream. It quickly floated away.

'I meant for you to keep hold of one end,' said the pixie.

'Then you should have said so,' replied the Prince.

'Do you have anything that floats?' asked the pixie. 'If you throw it into the water I will be able to grab hold of it and make my way to the bank.'

The Prince threw all his most treasured possessions into the water. His sword didn't float and neither did his pet rock. Finally he threw his guitar in. It bobbed along like a boat and the pixie climbed aboard, making his way to the bank.

When the tiny pixie was dry and had regained his breath, he thanked Prince Horace for saving his life.

'I am true to my word,' said the pixie. 'You shall have whatever you desire. What will it be?'

The Prince thought as hard as he could. After four hours he said, 'A sandwich.'

The pixie was slightly puzzled. 'Why a sandwich?'

'I'm hungry. You see, my father the King has thrown me out of the castle because he says I am sappy.'

'He may be right,' said the pixie. 'I offer you the world and you ask for a sandwich.'

'Well, what *should* I wish for?' asked Prince Horace.

'What about gold or diamonds or a beach house?'

'All I want is for my father to be proud of me so he will let me back into the castle,' said Horace sadly.

'Then that should be your wish, you ningnong! And the best way to make your father proud will be to slay the dragon and claim that rich reward he keeps going on about.'

'What a good idea!' said the Prince, impressed.

'And the best way for you to do *that* is to stick me in your ear!'

The Prince didn't think this was quite as good as the other idea, but he did as the pixie told him.

Nestled in Horace's ear, the pixie gave the Prince directions on how to find the dragon. 'Just follow the sound of agonised screaming!' he said cheerfully.

Eventually they came to a small village that was being terrorised by a ferocious beast. From behind a barrel they watched a huge emerald dragon pick up a knight with its claws and squash him.

Prince Horace immediately had second thoughts about his wish. 'Look, just give me a sandwich and we'll forget all about the dragon,' he said.

'Hush!' said the pixie in his ear. 'Watch closely! We may learn how to destroy the monster.'

The dragon wrapped the knight in a big piece of seaweed and then started to eat him with chopsticks.

'Aha!' said the pixie. 'He has turned the knight into sushi. That means he is an oriental dragon. They are the fiercest of all.'

'Oh, great!' said Horace.

'However, I have travelled the world and I know a way to defeat him. Just do exactly what I say. Leap in front of the dragon and hold your hands out as though they are deadly weapons.'

'*What?*' gasped the Prince.

'Just do it. And it would help if you could make a loud noise like a cat being trodden on.'

Once again Prince Horace did as the pixie told him. When he leaped in front of the oriental dragon and posed with his arms held out, the dragon immediately dropped what it was eating and held up its fearsome claws in a similar pose.

THE SAPPY PRINCE

'Aaauuuughhhhhh!' yelled the dragon, the drool dripping from its razor-sharp fangs.

'Any more bright ideas?' Prince Horace asked the pixie in his ear.

'Jump up in the air, spin around and kick him on the nose!'

'He'll burn my leg off, you dodo!'

'Oriental dragons can't breathe fire,' advised the pixie. 'That's why they eat their food raw.'

Before long Horace and the dragon were leaping through the air, kicking out with their legs, chopping with their arms and shouting 'Aaauuuughhhhhh!' Even though the dragon was much bigger and fiercer than Horace, the young Prince was nimbler, and the pixie knew some neat tricks, such as the *Bong-Gerk* (Wing Leg Block) and the *Chin-Gum-Sau* (Front Pinning Hand). The dragon was finally knocked out by an expert *Bui-Tze-Chin-Tek* (Kick in the Guts).

'Now you must cut off the dragon's head,' said the pixie.

'Er, yes,' said Prince Horace.

'What are you waiting for?'

'Well, I haven't cut off many dragons' heads before.'

'There's nothing to it!' said the pixie. 'Come on, you won't get your father's reward if you don't bring him the head.'

'Couldn't I just bring him a couple of scales or a toenail or something?'

'I don't think your dad will be very impressed by that.'

The dragon woke up and regarded the Prince with its oriental eyes.

'Why haven't you cut my head off yet?' it demanded, with subtitles.

'I've only got a pocket-knife and it might take quite a while,' said Prince Horace.

'Well, for heaven's sake get on with it!' said the dragon. 'You have beaten me fair and square. Now you have to chop my head off. That's the rule.'

Prince Horace took out his pocket-knife, which was one of those fancy models with about a dozen different attachments. The first one he flipped out was a screwdriver.

'Look, you can't screw my head off!' scolded the dragon. 'I'm not some robot monster from a Japanese movie!'

The Prince agreed that a screwdriver wasn't the ideal tool for removing a dragon's head. The next attachment he found was a nail file.

'Oh this is ridiculous!' snapped the dragon. 'You're going to *manicure* my head off?'

The pixie in Prince Horace's ear was feeling a little embarrassed. 'Try the hacksaw,' he suggested.

'Let's forget this whole head-cutting-off business,' said the Prince. 'It's far too yucky.'

'But I ate your mother and you must have your revenge on me!' reasoned the dragon.

'Yes, well, in that case I shall scold you severely,' said the Prince, putting away his pocket-knife. 'It was *very rude* of you to eat my mother and I'll be quite irritated if you ever do it again.'

'That's *it?*' said the dragon and the pixie together.

'I'm not much good at scolding,' admitted the Prince. 'And to be honest, my mother could be quite annoying. She was always droning on about manners.'

'That's true!' said the dragon. 'You should have heard the fuss she made when I ate her! She was cross with me for not using a napkin!'

'And she wouldn't shut up about it when I bounced on the bed,' said the Prince. 'I suppose I shouldn't have. At least, not while she was in it. But she went on and on!'

'You know, I've taken quite a shine to you,'

said the dragon. 'You're not bad for an idiot.'

'And you're not bad for a hideous non-fire-breathing monster,' replied the Prince.

'Call me Lee,' said the dragon.

And a true friendship was born.

That afternoon Horace returned to the castle.

'Hello!' he called. 'Anyone home?'

The King stuck his head out of the highest window and frowned when he saw his son. 'What are you doing back so soon, pea-head?'

'It is good to see you too, father,' replied Prince Horace. 'I've done something to make you proud. I have brought you the head of the fierce dragon that claimed my mother's life!'

'Why, this is wonderful news!' cried the King.

'Only I brought it with the body still attached,' said Prince Horace.

THE SAPPY PRINCE

Lee the dragon padded out from behind the rock where he had been hiding, and bowed.

'You've brought back a live dragon to the castle?' yelled the King in disbelief.

'Hi, Your Majesty!' called Lee the dragon. 'Sorry about eating your wife.'

'He's quite nice, really,' said Prince Horace. 'And he can't breathe fire so he won't burn anything down.'

'Your son is a good lad,' cried Lee the dragon. 'He spared my life, and in return I will bring you good fortune with my exotic dancing.'

'That's the stupidest thing I've ever heard!' yelled the King.

'Oh, and by the way I've got a little man in my ear,' said Horace.

'I was wrong,' said the King. '*That's* the stupidest thing I've ever heard.'

After some convincing, the King finally let his son Horace and Lee the dragon into the castle.

'You are castle-trained, I hope?' the King asked the dragon.

'Don't be rude to Lee!' said Prince Horace.

The King sighed. 'Very well, Horace. Here is your rich reward for bringing the head of the dragon. Even if you've brought some other bits as well that I don't particularly want.'

The King handed his son $7.50.

'*This* is my rich reward?' gulped Horace.

'Do you have any idea how much it costs to run a castle?' moaned the King. 'The gas bills alone are a nightmare. And I've just spent a fortune on chlorine for the moat. It was really starting to stink.'

'Never mind,' said Prince Horace. 'I'm happy to be back. Come on, Lee, let's bounce on the bed.'

The pixie decided to continue living in Horace's ear (provided Horace kept it clean and didn't charge rent) so he could teach the young Prince more about the world.

Gradually the sappy Prince became a very smart Prince indeed. He learned that castles make good tourist attractions. Before long the place was full of holidaymakers going on rides and paying to watch Lee the dragon do his exotic dancing - which really wasn't that great, but when you're a tourist you'll pay for anything.

Prince Horace even made up a special new song that he sang to all the visitors:

'Come and see our castle!
You're bound to get a thrill!
And never plump for second-best
When third is cheaper still!'

The moral of this story is: The pen is mightier than the sword, although I would prefer to be held up by someone with a pen.

The Gingerbread Mane

Once upon a time there was a teenage girl called Nana. She was quite short and totally bald. Nana's parents were also bald, but that was because the father was forty and the mother was a biker skinhead.

There is nothing wrong with being bald, and Nana had a sweet nature, but some children were mean to her. 'Yah! Boo!' the stupid children would chant. *'Na-na, Na-na, bald as a koala!'* Now, this doesn't even rhyme, and everyone knows koalas aren't bald at all, which just goes to show how stupid the children were.

Poor little Nana was terribly upset. She decided she would hide her baldness under a big hat, so she went to a shop that had the biggest range of hats in the land. Unfortunately it was run by a hatter who was mad, and who had escaped from another story.

'What can I do for you, young lady?' asked the hatter, as he enjoyed his morning cup of compost.

'I need a hat to disguise my bald noggin,' said Nana.

'This one is on special today,' said the hatter. He showed Nana a papery thing that was making a buzzing noise.

'Isn't that a wasps' nest?' asked Nana.

'Well, yes, but if you wear it on your head people won't notice you're bald. They'll be too busy dodging wasps.'

'I was really after something more hat-like,' said Nana.

'What about this one over here?' suggested the hatter. And he showed Nana the most beautiful hat she had ever seen. It was covered in feathers and magnificent jewels and wax fruit. The trouble was, there was a lady under it.

'Doesn't that hat already belong to that lady?' asked Nana.

'Oh, don't worry about her,' said the hatter.

'That's just my mother. She comes with the hat.'

'Can I buy the hat without the mother under it?'

'No, I'm afraid I can't separate them,' said the hatter.

Nana was losing patience. 'Do you have any *ordinary* hats that I might buy?'

'What about a nice bowler?' suggested the hatter.

'That's more like it!'

And the hatter introduced her to a Pakistani cricketer called Ahmed.

'I think I might go now,' said Nana.

When Nana was back home again, she decided on another plan. 'I will buy some hair from someone and stick it on my own head!' she said, proud of her clever idea.

The one girl in town who had more hair than anyone else was Rapunzel, a peculiar child who lived at the top of a tower. When Nana went to visit her, Rapunzel had hung her hair out of the window to dry.

'Hello, Rapunzel!' said Nana. 'Might I buy some of your hair to wear on my head, please?'

'Oh, you don't want *my* hair!' said Rapunzel. 'It's annoying stuff.'

'How do you mean?'

'Well, all these men keep climbing up it. Just look out the window!'

Nana peered out of Rapunzel's tower window and saw that there were indeed half a dozen men climbing up her hair.

'I have a better idea,' said Rapunzel. 'If you

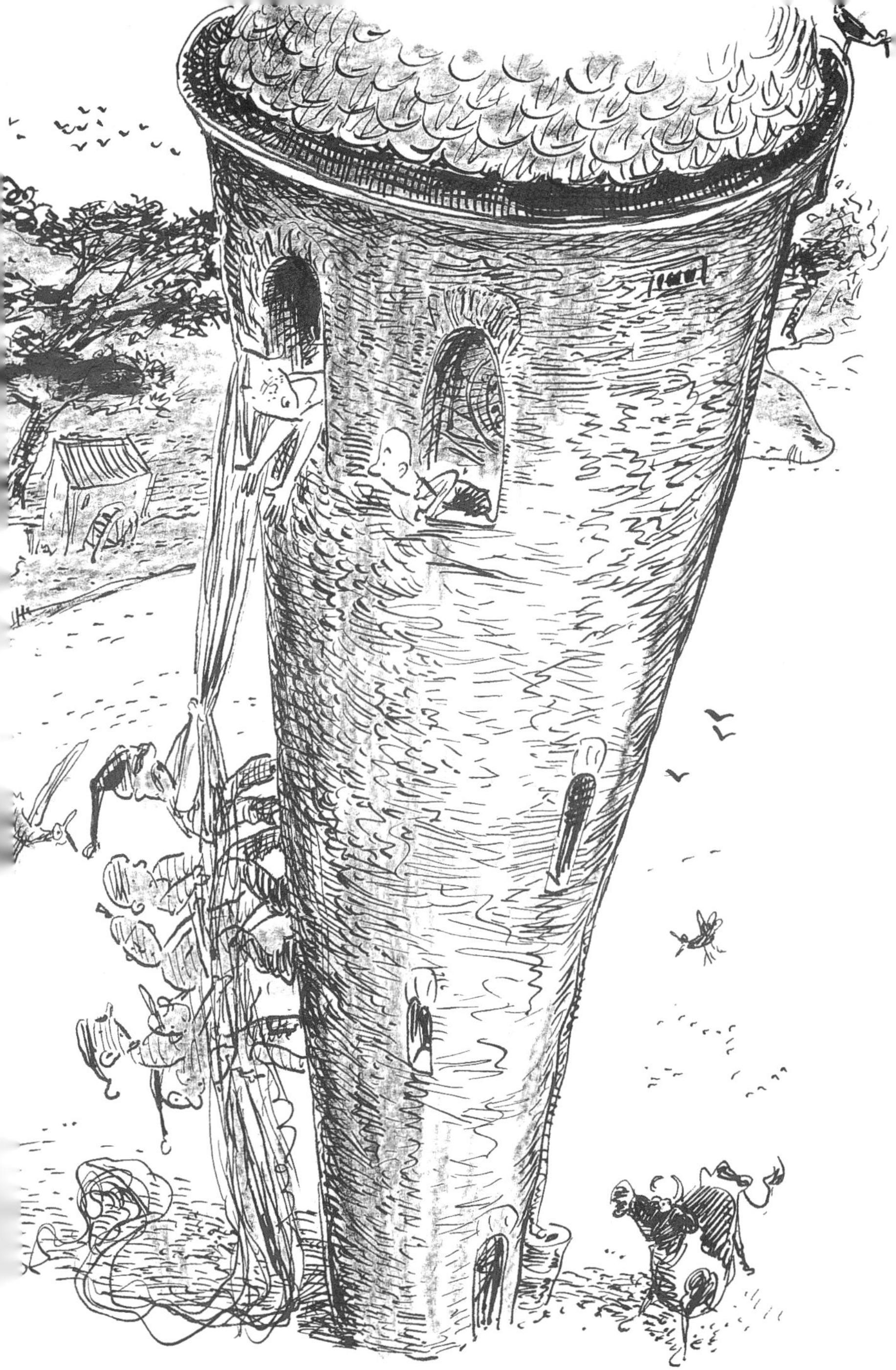

do as I say, you will never have to worry about being bald again.'

However, before she could say another word, she went flying out the window as all the men plummeted to the ground.

And so Nana returned home, as sad and bald as ever. Her mother tried to make her happy by singing songs, but the only ones she knew were skinhead ones like 'If You're Happy and You Know It, Bang Your Head', and Nana wasn't cheered up at all. Her father tried to make her happy by setting off fireworks, but he did it inside the house and burned down the spare room. This didn't cheer up Nana either, since that was where she slept.

On Saturday morning Nana's mum was making little gingerbread men to serve to the Hell's Angels who came around to afternoon tea every weekend. As Nana helped to roll out the gingerbread dough to cut into the little man shapes, she had an idea. When her mum's back was turned, Nana cut the dough into long strips and stuck it all to her head. It looked like a long mane of hair, the sort a strange lion might have.

'I'm not bald any more!' cried Nana, running around the house in delight, her gingerbread

mane flowing behind her.

'Your gingerbread mane is all very well,' said Nana's mother, 'but now I have nothing to serve to the Hell's Angels for afternoon tea. I'll have to give them something or they'll get cross and bust the telly. You must go to the baker's shop, Nana, and buy some buns.'

Nana ran all the way across town, proudly showing off her gingerbread mane as it flapped in the wind. When she arrived at the baker's shop she was completely out of breath and panted loudly.

'What big pants!' cried the baker.

Nana was about to tell the baker not to be so rude. But then she noticed that he looked very handsome in his smart baker's cap, so she smiled and tossed her gingerbread locks.

'I need ten dollars' worth of buns, please,' said Nana.

'Certainly,' said the baker. 'And may I ask your name?'

'It is Nana. You can call me Nan for short.'

'My name is Titus,' said the baker. 'You can't call me anything for short.' And he got the buns and started to wrap them.

Now, Titus the baker didn't go out much, and he thought Nana was the loveliest girl he had ever seen. But he was too shy to tell her, so he secretly wrote a love poem on the wrapping paper. It turned out to be quite a long poem, and by the time he had wrapped it around the buns the whole parcel was as big as an elephant.

When Nana got home with the enormous parcel, she unwrapped it and was amazed to see the love poem from Titus the baker. It stretched all the way from the hallway to the henhouse. One verse of the poem was so beautiful it made Nana burst into tears:

When you gaze upon my cakes,
What a noise my poor heart makes!
Bing and bang and bop and boo!
Baby I'm in love with you!

'What is this romantic poetry doing all over the place?' demanded Nana's mum.

'It's from the baker,' said Nana. 'I think he's in love with me.'

'And do you love him back?' asked Nana's mum.

'I do have a funny feeling deep down,' said Nana. 'But I've eaten half the buns so it might be tummy-ache.'

'It is love,' said Nana's mum. 'Jump on my Harley motorbike and go to him, my bald bambino!'

Nana did exactly as her mother said, and rode the enormous bike through the peak hour

traffic. Then something dreadful happened. There was a crash of thunder, and rain started to pour. When Nana finally reached the baker's shop the rain had washed away her gingerbread mane and she was bald again. She burst into tears.

'Poor Nan,' Titus said, sweetly. 'Why do you cry?'

'Because I'm as bald as a googy-egg!' said Nana.

'But I knew that already!' he said.

'Didn't you think I had a lovely long mane of hair?' she asked.

'No, I'm a baker. I know what gingerbread dough looks like. I was concerned that you had it on your head. But now I see you are quite normal and I love you more than ever.'

With that, Titus took off his smart baker's cap to reveal that he too was completely bald. If anything, Nana thought it made him look even more handsome.

'Will you marry me?' asked Nana.

'Yes!' said Titus. 'And I will make a wedding cake with two little bald people on top.'

So bald Nana and bald Titus the baker got married. All the Hell's Angels came, and so did the mad hatter, wearing a wasps' nest on his head, and so did Rapunzel, dragging a whole bunch of climbers behind her. When the climbers saw the huge wedding cake they decided to leave poor Rapunzel's hair alone and climb the cake instead.

Everyone agreed that it was the best wedding they had ever been to, except there were probably too many wasps.

The moral of this story is: You can't have your cake and eat it too. You shouldn't really climb it, either. Marzipan avalanches can be quite dangerous.

Goldilocks and The Three Beards

Once upon a time there was a rock band called The Three Beards. It was hugely popular and the musicians rehearsed regularly in a mansion in the forest. One reason why the band was so popular was that the players were all very mysterious, with beards so enormous that nobody knew who was behind them.

Not far away from the forest lived an annoying girl called Goldilocks who wanted to be a rock star. She didn't really have blonde hair. And her real name was Beverly Winterbottom, which isn't a good name for a rock star, so she changed it. She had a strange tattoo around her arm. The tattooist, who did not like Goldilocks, had told her it was old-fashioned writing that meant *girl power*, although it actually meant *bush pig*.

Now, Goldilocks had read in popular magazines that many famous rock stars are very badly behaved, so she always left her old underpants lying all over the place. 'That is what rock stars do,' she said when her parents, Mr and Mrs Winterbottom, complained. She kicked the telly out of the window. 'This is also what rock stars do,' she said. At tea time she threw her food at the wall, or arranged the letters in her alphabet soup to form swearwords.

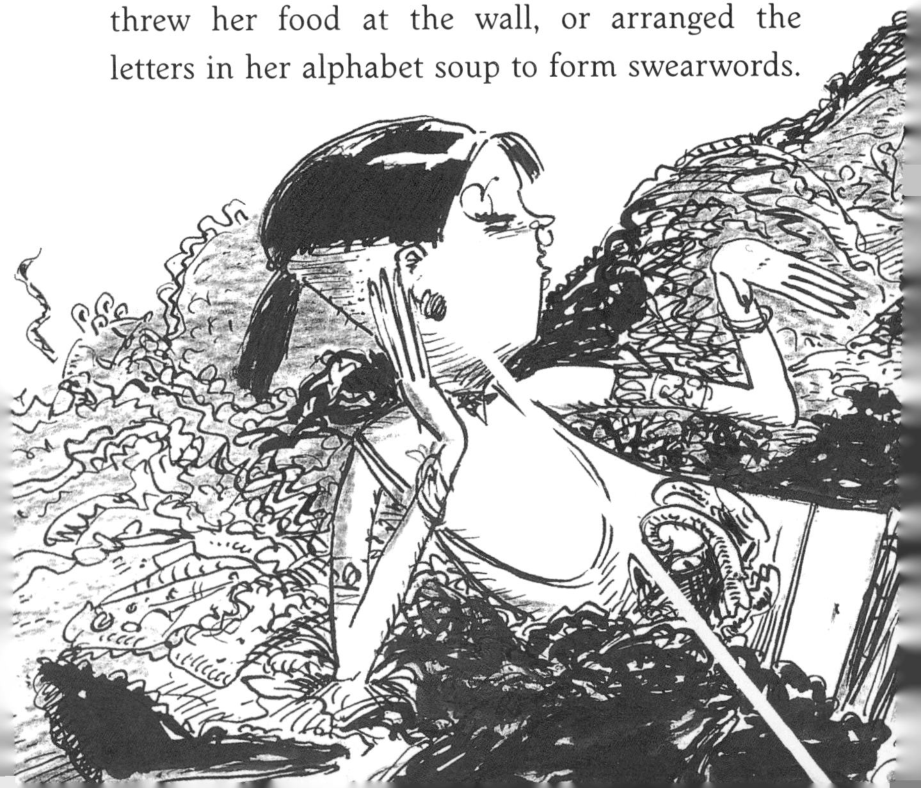

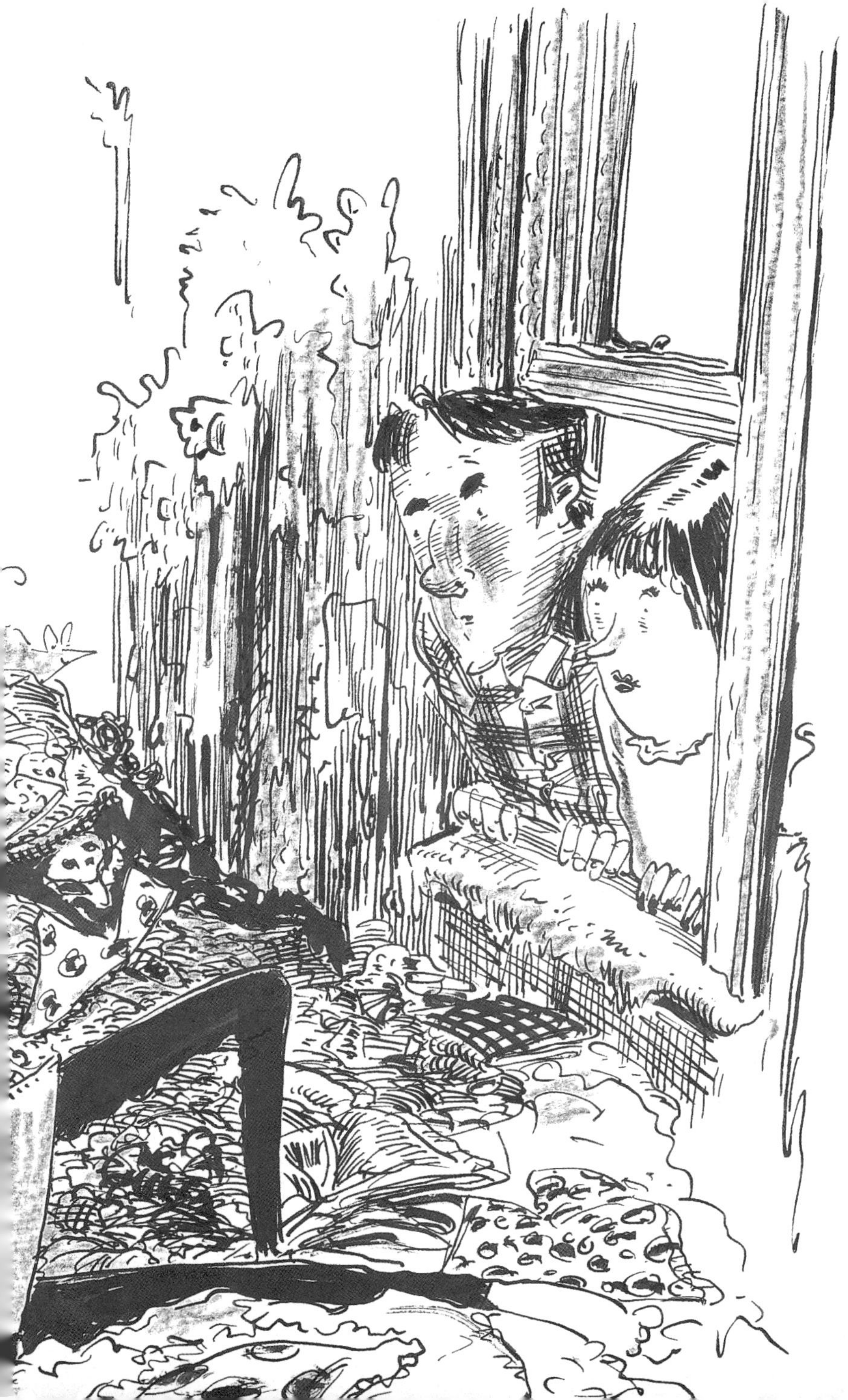

The troublesome child sang very bad rock songs morning, noon and night, and her parents hated it. Mr and Mrs Winterbottom didn't want their daughter to be a rock star. They wanted her to be a nuclear scientist and split atoms.

'Poo!' said Goldilocks. 'I don't want to split atoms! I might blow myself up.' This, of course, is what her parents were hoping would happen.

The teachers at Goldilocks's school disliked her so much that they often stayed at home. Their parents were always writing sick notes to say why the teachers weren't at school today.

Goldilocks was cheeky to all the staff. When Mr Brown the maths teacher asked her what you got if you added 437 to 139, Goldilocks replied, 'Bored.' When Mr White the French teacher asked her what was the most famous building in Paris, she said, 'The Awful Tower.' And when Mr Beige the trigonometry teacher asked her what was the hypotenuse of an equilateral triangle, she just told him to get nicked.

'You must study harder, Goldilocks,' said the Principal, 'or you will have to stay down yet again. You're still only in Year Two and that's not good for a sixteen-year-old.'

GOLDILOCKS AND THE THREE BEARDS

'Poo!' cried Goldilocks. 'I don't need to study, for I am going to be a rock star and I will be on the cover of a magazine, which is something that will never happen to you because you are too boring!'

The Principal burst into tears.

Goldilocks thought that a quick way of becoming a rock star would be to go on a TV talent quest.

Two judges watched and listened as Goldilocks danced about and sang a song she had written all by herself. Then the presenter of the show turned to the judges and asked them for their opinion.

'Well, you have a nice voice,' said judge one.
'*Very* nice voice!' said judge two.
'And you're rather attractive,' said judge one.
'*Extremely* attractive!' said judge two.
'And your personality is bright and sunny,' said judge one.
'*Very* bright and *extremely* sunny!' said judge two.
'In fact you're very talented indeed!' said both judges.
'Thank you very much,' said Goldilocks.

'We weren't talking about you, we were talking about the presenter,' said the judges.

'Oh,' said Goldilocks. 'What do you think of *me*?'

'You're rubbish,' said the judges.

But Goldilocks was still determined to be a rock star. She dreamed of what it must be like in the mansion in the forest where The Three Beards rehearsed. She was sure the floor would be knee-deep in old underpants and there would be food all over the walls and the garden would be full of busted tellies. It all seemed very romantic to her. So one day she decided to break into the mansion. There was a sign on the door saying PLEASE DON'T BREAK INTO THIS MANSION, but Goldilocks couldn't read it and would have ignored it even if she could.

Wicked Goldilocks walked around the big deserted mansion. She didn't see a single pair of underpants on the floor. There was no food on the walls. There was only one television and it was a plasma one that was far too big to kick out of the window.

'Poo! This doesn't look like a rock star house at all!' she sniffed. 'I will have to do something about that!'

In the kitchen there were three bowls of porridge. Goldilocks threw them all at the wall. In the sitting room there were three chairs. Goldilocks pulled them apart. And in the bedroom there were three beds. Goldilocks bounced on them all so hard that she hit her head on the ceiling and knocked herself out.

The Three Beards came to the mansion that night to rehearse, and found that their lovely place had been trashed.

'Someone's been throwing porridge at the wall!' said Beard Number One.

'Someone's pulled apart our Swedish furniture that we made from a kit!' said Beard Number Two.

'Someone's been bouncing on the beds and she's asleep on the doona!' said Beard Number Three.

The Three Beards shook the bed angrily until Goldilocks fell off.

'What are you doing in our mansion?' demanded Beard Number One.

'None of your beeswax,' said Goldilocks. 'And I will not leave until you give me a job.'

Beard Number Two nodded thoughtfully. 'We will only give you a job if you clean up all the mess you have made.'

'And you can unblock the loo while you're about it,' said Beard Number Three.

Goldilocks had never done any cleaning in her life, but she was so determined to be a rock star that she decided to get to work. She scraped the porridge off the wall. She put the Swedish

furniture back together in about fifteen hours, which is how long it usually takes. She fixed up the crack her head had made in the bedroom ceiling and she even unblocked the loo.

Then Goldilocks told The Three Beards she had cleaned up all the mess and was now ready to join their band. But The Three Beards just laughed at her and removed their large false beards to reveal Mr Brown, Mr White and Mr Beige.

'You're not rock stars!' gasped Goldilocks. 'You're schoolteachers!'

'And proud of it!' said Mr Brown the maths teacher. 'For we wouldn't be rock stars if we couldn't add up.'

'Nor if we didn't know about France,' said Mr White the French teacher.

'Nor if we didn't know that the square of the hypotenuse of a triangle is equal to the sum of the squares of the other two sides,' said Mr Beige the trigonometry teacher.

'But you told me you would offer me a job!' complained Goldilocks.

'And so we shall! You can be our permanent loo-unblocker.'

'Poo! I have been tricked!' cried Goldilocks.

'And you have given us a wonderful idea for our new rock song,' said Mr Brown. 'It's called "Rack Off, Goldilocks, We'd Prefer Chickenpox"!'

The song became a huge hit. Goldilocks refused to be a loo-unblocker and went off to be a nuclear scientist instead. But because she didn't have the qualifications she did indeed blow herself up and both her parents were quite happy.

And the Principal *did* get on the cover of a magazine when he won the Mr Universe body-building contest, so he was quite happy too.

The moral of this story is: Slow and steady wins the race, unless it is the Grand Prix. In which case, go like stink.

Pansel and Grekel

Once upon a time there lived a poor woodcutter with his new wife and his two children. The children were twins, even though they were born three months apart. The boy was called Pansel and the girl Grekel, so they copped a fair bit of teasing. But they were both sweet children and the father loved them dearly. The stepmother, however, did not like the children at all, for she was wicked, like most stepmothers in fairytales.

The poor woodcutter found it harder and harder to get work because he had chopped down most of the trees in the area. He had so little money that he couldn't put food on the table. (This was because he'd sold the table.)

Neither could he afford to buy shoes for Pansel and Grekel to go to school, especially as they wanted those fancy new cross-trainers with the integrated lacing system.

'Do not worry, father,' said Pansel happily. 'We just won't go to school.'

But the woodcutter was having none of it. He made his children some cross-trainers out of wood and they copped even more teasing.

One morning, after the woodcutter left for work, the stepmother took Pansel and Grekel to Big Fat Enormous World, which was the largest supermarket in the universe. There were huge checkouts with toys and lollies so all the children would scream their lungs out for them as their parents queued to pay for the groceries.

Now, the stepmother had no money, but she had not gone to Big Fat Enormous World to buy stuff. She had gone there to lose the children. 'Heh heh heh!' she said. Pansel suspected she might be up to something wicked, especially when she kept saying, 'Heh heh heh!'

While the stepmother's back was turned, Pansel went to a lady who was handing out free samples of salami and he took the lot, stuffing it in his pockets.

As the stepmother led Pansel and Grekel further and further into the depths of the supermarket, Pansel dropped a trail of salami. Next thing the children knew, their stepmother had left them, believing she would be rid of them for good. However, Pansel and Grekel found their way out by following the pieces of salami, carefully stepping over all the people who had slipped on them.

So Pansel and Grekel arrived home again a few hours later. The stepmother pretended to be happy to see them. The woodcutter was so relieved that he hugged his children tight.

'Children, where have you been?' he asked. 'And why do you both stink to high heaven?'

Pansel and Grekel explained about their adventure with the salami. The woodcutter listened while the stepmother just smiled sweetly and continued throwing darts at the children's school photos.

The next time the stepmother took the children to Big Fat Enormous World she made sure there was no one handing out free samples of anything. She left Pansel and Grekel in Aisle

Nine, which is that weird aisle that contains all the stuff that doesn't quite belong in the other aisles. There were huge bags of kitty litter and garden hoses and rubber gloves and old-fashioned video cassettes. It was a dreadful place and hardly anyone went there.

This time the children really *were* lost. They roamed around trying to find a way out, but kept coming back to the same spot. Before they knew it, the supermarket was closed.

'How will we spend the night?' gasped Grekel. 'We have nothing but the clothes we wear and these stupid wooden cross-trainers. We will surely starve!'

They knew it was a crime to steal the food from the shelves, but they were both so hungry that they decided it would be all right if they took eight items or less.

After eating eight roast chooks and eight packets of chocolate biscuits, the children again tried to find their way out of the enormous supermarket, but found themselves back in dreaded Aisle Nine.

'I have an idea!' said Pansel. 'We can unwind all the tape from a video cassette and trail it behind us, and that way we will know if we have passed that way before!'

They unravelled a video cassette called *Sing with The Puffles* and soon they had wound it around every single shelf. The videotape stretched and stretched and before long all the shelves came crashing down.

The supermarket manager was furious when he arrived the next morning to see his trashed supermarket. By following the *Puffles* tape he eventually found Pansel and Grekel, covered in bits of chocolate biscuit and chicken. He asked them where they lived and then contacted the stepmother.

Three days later she came to collect the children.

'Thank you, kind sir,' said the stepmother to the manager. 'Now, come home with me, dear

Handbag and Grovel.' (She often got the children's names wrong because she hated them so much.)

'Not so fast!' said the manager. 'I will not let you leave until you pay for *Sing with The Puffles*. Somebody has to.'

The evil stepmother coughed up what little money she had because she was afraid the cops would come.

Pansel gathered up all the tape and stuck it back in the cassette.

The stepmother decided to abandon the whole supermarket idea, and the next day she left Pansel and Grekel in a multi-storey car park instead. They were lost again, but smart little Grekel hot-wired an old car and managed to drive them both out. They were pulled over by a police officer.

'What are you two kids doing driving around in this car?' he demanded.

'Leave it to me,' whispered Grekel to Pansel.

'Well?' said the police officer. 'Answer my question!'

'This car belongs to me!' said Grekel grandly.

'And how old are you, young lady?'

'Eighty-three and fourteen months,' said Grekel.

'And how did you come to have a car like this?'

'Tarzan gave it to me when I rescued him from quicksand,' said Grekel.

'And do you have a driver's licence?' asked the police officer.

'I have three,' said Grekel.

'May I see them?'

'No, you may not. Two of them were eaten by a walking fish and the other one was carried off by killer bees,' said Grekel.

'And is there anyone who will back up your story?' asked the police officer.

'Yes, but he's invisible,' said Grekel.

'And how would I get in touch with him?'

'Easily,' said Grekel. 'He lives in your trousers.'

'Well, everything seems to be in order here,' said the police officer. He jumped back into his squad car, turned the siren on and got home just in time for his favourite soap opera.

The woodcutter was starting to get suspicious. One night he had a chat with the stepmother.

'You seem to be losing the children quite often,' he said. 'Are you doing it on purpose?'

'What a terrible thing to say!'

'You took them to the beach and they were swept half way to New Zealand.'

'It was their fault for not swimming between the flags.'

'You buried the flags,' said the woodcutter. 'And the children say you pushed them off the end of the pier.'

'Piffle!' said the stepmother. 'I *adore* the children. Only last week I gave them a lovely game of snakes and ladders.'

'With live snakes,' said the woodcutter.

'I thought it would be more educational,' said the stepmother.

'I see. And tell me, dearest, what are the children's names?' asked the woodcutter cunningly.

'Their names?'

'Yes.'

The stepmother thought hard. 'Why, Handle and Kettle of course!'

'Wrong.'

'Bangle and Spittle?'

'Wrong again.'

'Dangle and Freckle?'

'If you truly loved them you would know their names are Pansel and Grekel.'

'That was my next guess!' said the stepmother.

But the woodcutter was having none of it. 'Today I watched that video you got from the supermarket,' he said. 'It wasn't *Sing with The Puffles* at all. It was the videotape from a supermarket security camera. It quite clearly showed you abandoning the children in terrible Aisle Nine.'

Clever Pansel had swapped the tapes around so now there was proof of the stepmother's villainy.

The woodcutter chucked out the wicked stepmother and found new work in the building industry. Since there was hardly any wood left, people were now building houses out of gingerbread.

One day Pansel and Grekel started eating one of these houses. The witch who lived there got rather annoyed about it, especially as they ate her bathroom, but that's another story. It's called *Pansel and Grekel and the Annoyed Smelly Witch* and it's probably available in Aisle Nine at your local supermarket.

The moral of this story is: There is more than one way to skin a cat, but they're all pretty disgusting.

Snow White and the Seventy Dwarfs

Once upon a time a Queen sat sewing by a window in the northern tower of her castle. The birds were twittering in the trees and the morning sun was spreading its long golden fingers over the lush countryside.

'Good morning, birds! Good morning, trees!' called the happy Queen, whose name was Beryl.

Then the Queen mysteriously fell out the window and through the roof of an ice-cream van that was parked outside. She landed in a big churn of vanilla and was turned into a Dairy Queen.

The van drove away, leaving behind a

heartbroken King and a beautiful Princess called Snow White.

After a time the King took himself another wife, a noblewoman who already lived in the castle, quite near the northern tower actually. She too was beautiful, but she was also vain and couldn't bear people who might be prettier than she was. Indeed, she would secretly push them out of windows. (Smart readers may now have worked out that what happened to the first

Queen wasn't quite so mysterious after all.)

When this new Queen invited noblewomen around to tea parties, they tried to make themselves ugly by colouring their teeth with felt pens, or putting baked beans in their hair.

'You look quite *pretty*,' the Queen told a nervous young Duchess one afternoon.

'Oh, but I am not!' said the Duchess, squinting her eyes and sticking an apple in her mouth so she looked like a roast pig.

'But you have such nice hair!' said the Queen, jealously.

'It is a wig,' said the Duchess.

So the Queen pulled it off. It took some effort, as it really was the Duchess's hair, but it came off eventually.

Snow White looked after her father, the King, who'd become unwell. He had a rare disease that made him dance whenever he spoke. It was awkward to have a conversation with him because as soon as he opened his mouth he started jiving or doing the can-can. Now, the King was nearly eighty and far too old for jiving, let alone can-canning, so he spoke as little as possible and remained in bed.

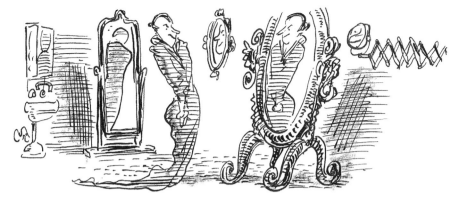

The Queen was too vain and mad to worry about the King. She had mirrors installed in every single room so she could always admire herself. Except in the toilet, of course. She wasn't quite *that* vain and mad. Her favourite mirror was a magic one that could answer all her questions, except ones about geography, which it wasn't good at. The Queen would ask it every day:

*'Mirror, mirror, on the wall,
Who's the biggest spunk there is?'*

The mirror answered her in rhyme:

*'You're the biggest spunk by far,
Queenie, baby, yes you are!'*

And the Queen was satisfied and gave her mad laugh: 'Hahahahahahahaha!'

Meanwhile, the King's condition grew worse.

'Snow White, my dear daughter, I think I am dying!' he said, doing the twist up and down his bedroom.

'Father, save your breath or you will twist yourself to death,' said Snow White.

'I worry about what will happen to you when I'm gone!' said the King, moon-walking into a vase.

'Get back into bed, Father!' said Snow White. 'If you want to tell me something then you must write it down.'

The King scribbled on a piece of paper: *Beware the Queen. She is mad.*

Snow White read the note and then knelt at her father's bedside. She took out a piece of paper and on it she wrote: *Do not worry, Father, I have a way of dealing with her.* Then she handed the note to her father.

What did you have in mind? wrote the King on another piece of paper.

Well, I thought I might throw a bucket of water over her and make her melt, Snow White wrote back.

What makes you think she'll melt? wrote the King on yet another piece of paper.

It happened in this story I read, wrote Snow White.

I've read that story too, wrote the King. *But it was a wicked witch who melted. The Queen is a human. If you throw a bucket of water over her she'll just get wet and probably quite stroppy.*

Oh dear! wrote Snow White. *If only Mother hadn't fallen out of that window and been turned into an ice cream!*

These things happen! wrote the King. *Now you'd better get rid of these notes or the Queen will find them and know we've been plotting against her.*

How do you think I should get rid of them all? wrote Snow White.

The safest way is to eat them, wrote the King.

What, every single one of them? wrote Snow White.

Yes, wrote the King, *for if the Queen finds just one tiny note she will know something is up and lose her marbles completely and take out a terrible revenge upon us both that I don't even dare to think about.*

In that case, wrote Snow White, *please stop writing such long notes because they'll be harder for me to eat.*

Sorry, wrote the King.

And Snow White sat down to eat an unpleasant meal of secret messages, but she didn't mind because she loved her father and would do anything for him. If only she could work out some way of curing his dreaded dancing disease!

Later that night, when Snow White passed the Queen in a corridor, she threw a bucket of water over her. There was no harm in trying, she thought.

Angrily the Queen threw a bucket of water straight back. 'Now you're Snow Wet!' laughed the Queen. 'Hahahahahahahaha!'

Despite her husband's illness, the nasty Queen

would not come to his bedside. Instead she spent her time gazing into her favourite mirror and asking it questions. Pretty soon she ran out of good questions to ask and this is the best she could come up with:

'Mirror mirror, on the wall,
What is the capital of Nigeria?'

The mirror was annoyed with the Queen because she already knew it couldn't answer questions about geography, so it decided to teach her a lesson. It answered:

'I don't know the capital of Nigeria, it's true,
But baby, I've got news for you!
Although you are a honey-bun,
They say Snow White's a bigger one!'

The Queen was enraged by the news. From that very hour, she hated Snow White.

Even the mad Queen was sensible enough to know she couldn't just push Snow White out the window because it was all starting to look a bit suspicious. So she called a huntsman and said, 'Take the girl into the forest. Kill her, and bring me back her heart! Hahahahahahahaha!'

The huntsman obeyed, even if this was a bit outside his usual line of work, and took Snow White away into the forest. But when he had drawn his knife, he decided he couldn't harm her because she was so beautiful. (This is one of the unfair things about the world. If the Princess had looked like a smashed yam in a frock the huntsman would have killed her, but he spared her life and released her because of her twinkly eyes and her enchanting bust.)

Remembering what the Queen had said, the hunter bought a beef heart at the supermarket. He took it to the Queen to prove Snow White was dead.

'Are you sure this is Snow White's heart?' asked the Queen.

'I swear to it,' said the huntsman.

'It is in a styrene tray and covered in cling wrap.'

'I thought Your Majesty would like me to present it like that, rather than drop a messy lump at your feet.'

'You are a wise and thoughtful huntsman,' said the Queen, 'though I'm still a bit suspicious about the sticker that says RED SPOT SPECIAL.'

'Er, it's a tribute to your beauty,' replied the huntsman, who was even worse at making up believable explanations than he was at killing Princesses.

'Hahahahahahahaha!' said the Queen. 'Sorry, I don't know why I laughed just then.'

When Snow White woke up in the deep dark forest, a funny little man in a waistcoat was leaning over her. He was holding a stinky flower under her nose.

'Who are you?' asked Snow White.

'My name is Blonk,' said the funny little man.

'Oh, I am very sorry about that,' said Snow White.

'Not as sorry as I am,' said Blonk.

'Why are you holding that stinky flower under my nose?'

'You passed out. My magic flower helped you to wake up.'

'Bull!' said Snow White.

'Dwarfs do not lie!' said Blonk proudly, standing up to his full height.

Snow White laughed at the funny little man, because she was young and innocent and didn't realise that it's rude to laugh at dwarfs unless they tell you jokes or tickle you.

Blonk led Snow White to the cottage where he lived with his brothers and cousins and friends.

'Behold my tiny home!' he cried. 'It has a tiny fence and a tiny chimney and a tiny letterbox and ...'

'I get the idea,' said Snow White. 'How many of you live here?'

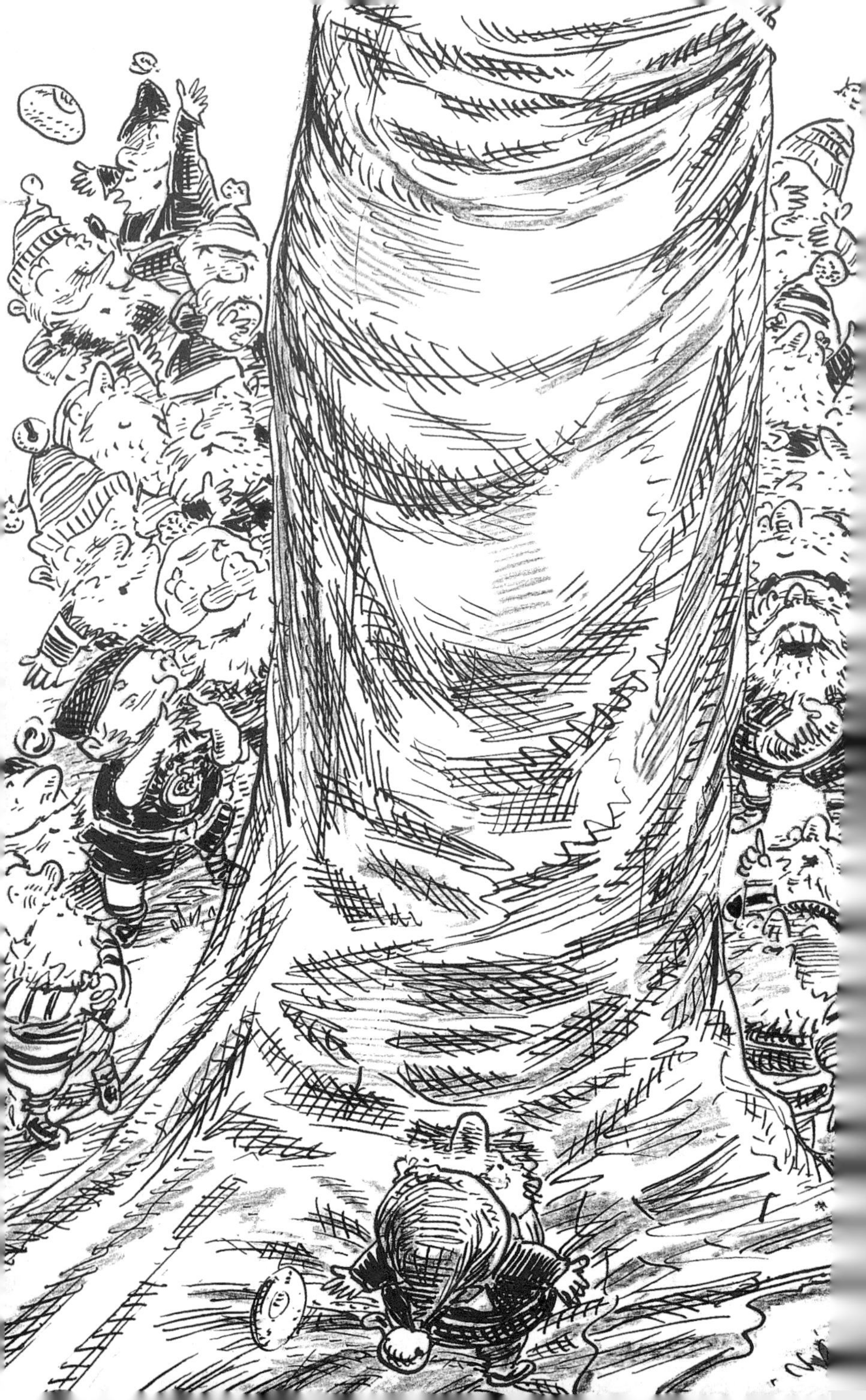

SNOW WHITE AND THE SEVENTY DWARFS

'Seventy,' said Blonk.

And lo and behold, the dwarfs came out to greet their pretty young guest.

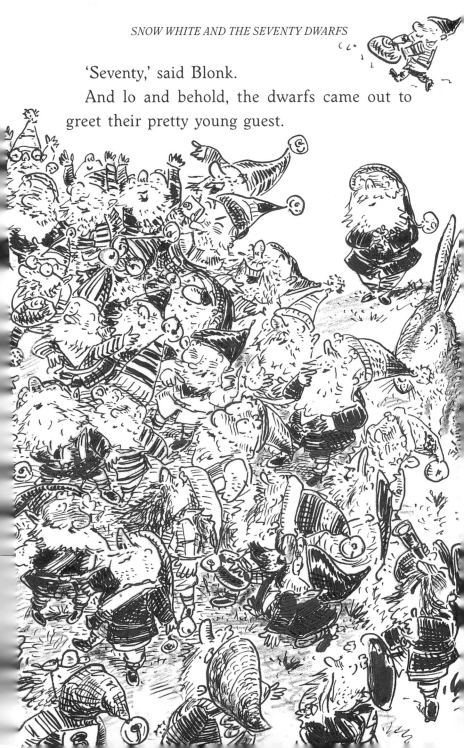

Besides Blonk there were Cheeky, Nosey, Awful, Pants, Kevin, Fatty, Muscles, Snotty, Pinhead, Parallelogram, Hokey, Pokey, Ipsy, Wipsy, Shoehorn, Teeny, Weeny, Bikini, Oogie, Woogie, Boogie, Patootie, Malcolm, Flipper, Hanky, Panky, Thumbprint, Blinky, Stinky, Andronicus, Wimpy, Jumpy, Creepy, Crawly, Flyboy, Lamington, Photocopy, Wrist, Puffy, Pastry, Marco, Rico, Hippo, Hoppo, Bumpo, Omo, Silt, Smartie, Mintie, Choo-choo, Glark, Glaaaaark, Glaaaaaaaaark, Pesticide, Wilberforce, Wombat, Phillip, Chooky, Scud, Tambourine, Ig, Fax, Hosiery, Lint, Sausagemince, Ringo, Butch, Peanut and Christopher.

'Hello, I'm Snow White,' said the visitor.

'What a strange name!' said Parallelogram.

The young Princess explained to Blonk about her father and the dreadful disease that was making him dance whenever he spoke. Would Blonk be able to cure him with his magic flower?

'Ah, now that is a toughie!' said Blonk. 'I can take the disease from your father but I must pass it on to someone else, for this disease cannot be destroyed, merely transferred.'

'Pass it on to me!' said Snow White. 'I am young and strong and do not mind if I dance about!'

Blonk was impressed by such a sweet gesture. He also quite liked the idea of Snow White dancing about. So they both went to the castle, even though it probably wasn't the safest place to be.

'Don't stand near any windows,' Snow White advised Blonk.

The mad Queen was surprised when Snow White broke into her private bedroom.

She was even more surprised when the back of Snow White's dress started moving around in a most peculiar way. Snow White had feared for Blonk's safety, so she had allowed the dwarf to hide under her gown. He was shivering with nerves.

'I come to save Father's life!' cried Snow White. 'And you can't stop me because I no longer fear you!'

'How did your bottom get so big all of a sudden?' asked the Queen curiously. 'And why is it jiggling up and down like that?'

'Never mind my bottom!' snapped Snow White. 'I just came to tell you that I know about your treachery, and your days are numbered!'

Under the dress Blonk sneezed. 'Sorry about that,' he said.

'Your father is in his bed,' said the Queen, still rather curious about the way Snow White's bottom was behaving. 'But you cannot save him. Last night when he said his prayers he did "The Time Warp" and he is now close to death. And when he is gone, I will rule the land so harshly that you'll wish that huntsman had killed you after all!'

'I go to Father!' cried Snow White.

'Hang on!' said the mad Queen. 'I haven't done my laugh yet. Hahahahahahahaha!'

Snow White pushed past the Queen and made for the King's bedside.

'Who is there?' the King asked weakly, his legs doing a few tired dance steps.

'Do not cha-cha, Father! It is your daughter Snow White and I have a dwarf who will make you well.'

Blonk pulled out the magic flower from his waistcoat and asked the King to breathe on it. Then he took the flower over to Snow White and asked her to sniff it, so the disease would move from one person to the other. But before Snow White had a chance, the mad Queen dashed into the room.

'You *dare* to offer Snow White a flower when *I* am the fairest in the land?'

The mad Queen snatched the flower from Blonk's hand.

'Poo! It smells like a school bus!' she said, suddenly breaking into a tap-dance.

The King was cured!

The Queen was in a foul mood because she now had the dancing disease. She shimmied off to glare at the magic mirror. It tried to calm her down by telling her the capital of Nigeria is Lagos.

'Shut up!' snarled the Queen, slam-dancing at the mirror and breaking it into a thousand pieces.

The King decided to hold a public ceremony to thank all the dwarfs. And because he was angry with the Queen, he made her read out the entire list of names.

The Queen took a deep breath, and then said, 'We wish to offer our thanks to Blonk, Cheeky, Nosey, Awful, Pants, Kevin, Fatty, Muscles, Snotty, Pinhead, Parallelogram, Hokey, Pokey, Ipsy, Wipsy, Shoehorn, Teeny, Weeny, Bikini, Oogie, Woogie, Boogie, Patootie, Malcolm, Flipper, Hanky, Panky, Thumbprint, Blinky, Stinky, Andronicus, Wimpy, Jumpy, Creepy, Crawly, Flyboy, Lamington, Photocopy, Wrist, Puffy, Pastry, Marco, Rico, Hippo, Hoppo, Bumpo, Omo, Silt, Smartie, Mintie, Choo-choo, Glark, Glaaaaark, Glaaaaaaaaaark, Pesticide, Wilberforce, Wombat, Phillip, Chooky, Scud, Tambourine, Ig, Fax, Hosiery, Lint, Sausagemince, Ringo, Butch, Peanut and Christopher.'

By the time she had finished reading the list the Queen had danced herself into jelly, and there was much rejoicing. As the happy crowd cheered and laughed, an ice-cream van drove up, its merry chimes lighting up the faces of the children. Everyone was amazed when out of the van stepped Snow White's mother, Queen Beryl. Snow White ran to embrace her.

'I thought you'd been turned into an ice cream and I'd never see you again!' cried Snow White joyously.

'I'm a bit surprised about that myself,' said Queen Beryl. 'Fortunately a wizard bought me and turned me back into a human by licking me.'

'But that's stupid!' said Snow White.

'Well, yes, it probably doesn't make a lot of sense,' agreed the Queen. 'But it's certainly no more stupid than Princesses kissing frogs, or pigs getting their houses blown down by wolves, or girls sleeping for a hundred years after pricking their fingers on spindles, or ...'

'I get the idea,' said Snow White.

Everyone was happy again and the dwarfs were all knighted for their good work. So their names were now Sir Blonk, Sir Cheeky, Sir Nosey, Sir Awful, Sir Pants, Sir Kevin, Sir Fatty, Sir Muscles, Sir Snotty, Sir Pinhead, Sir Parallelogram, Sir Hokey, Sir Pokey ...

You get the idea.

The moral of this story is: Laughter is the best medicine, unless you have diarrhoea, in which case you should stop laughing and take a tablet.

And the capital of Nigeria is Abuja, not Lagos, so it just goes to show that you should never believe everything talking mirrors tell you.

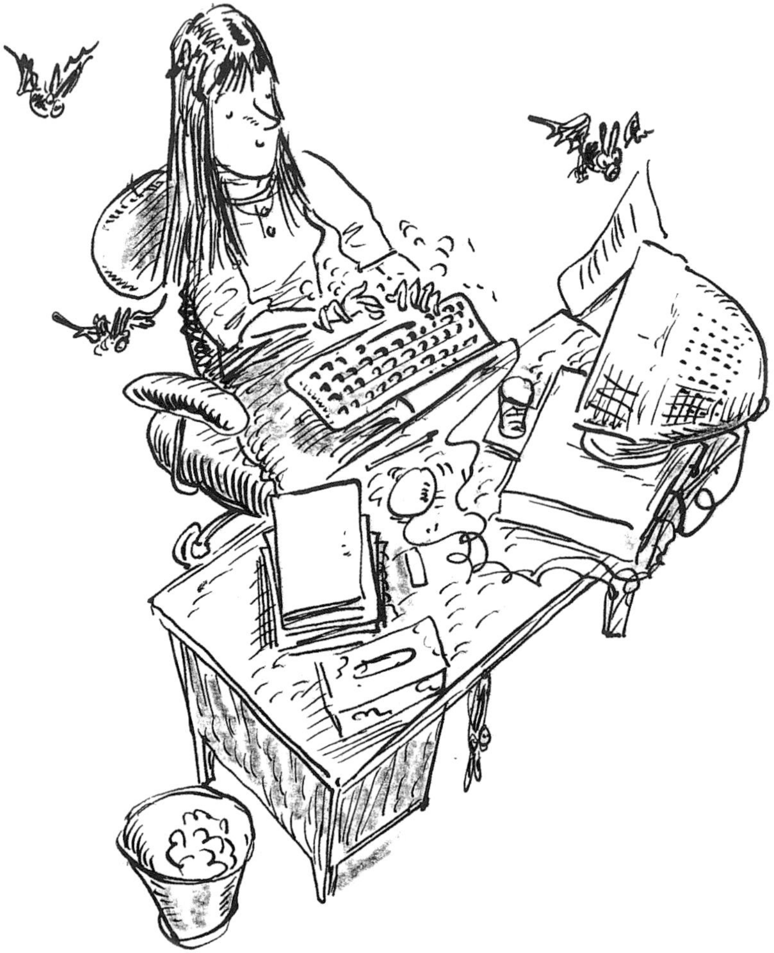

How it all ended

'We're very proud of this stupid book,' Una Spooner told the crowd of two reporters who had come to the official launch party for *Leon Stumble's Book of Stupid Fairytales.*

'Is it true the idea was yours?' asked the first reporter.

'Oh yes, it was entirely mine,' said Una. 'I'm full of stupid ideas.'

'And nobody else had a hand in it?' asked the second reporter.

'Well, the author did, slightly,' said Una. 'But he only wrote the book. The idea's the important thing. And I thought it up all by myself. It came to me while I was having a bath in Frankfurt. Or was I having a frankfurt in Bath? I can't remember now, but it was definitely my idea.'

'And do you have any comment to make about your hair?'

Una eyed the young reporter sternly. 'Why?'

'Well, it's suddenly turned into the shape of a chicken.'

Una reached up her hand with its long red fingernails to discover that her normally sensible

hair had indeed turned into the shape of a farmyard fowl.

'How odd!' she said.

She took a brush out of her expensive Italian handbag and struggled to pull her hair back into its regular style, but no matter how hard she tried, it remained in the shape of a chicken.

'I shall be having a stern word with my hairdresser about this!'

'I think it just made a clucking noise,' said the second reporter.

'Oh, don't be ridiculous!' snapped Una, as an egg popped out of the back of her unusual new hairdo.

Cassie, standing nearby, was annoyed by Una's lies. After all, the book had most definitely been Cassie's idea. And even though witches are only supposed to use their power for good, Cassie bent the rules slightly by giving Una her interesting new hairstyle.

Leon looked thoughtful. Since writing his latest book, he had come to realise that there really was magic in the world after all. Leon was already thinking about his next book, which would be a practical guide on how to live with a witch. He hadn't told Cassie yet, but recently he had worked out her secret.

Now that he was no longer quite so caught up in educational writing, Leon had spent some time thinking about the peculiar things that had been going on. Yes, the furniture at home did seem to hover about, and desktop flowers did sometimes change into massive creeping vines when Cassie was around. But what made Leon wake up to the fact that Cassie might have magic powers was the way she used his computer.

It had happened just before the book was finished. When Leon's hands became too tired to type, Cassie took over at the keyboard. Leon dictated his stupid stories about dancing dragons and girls with gingerbread hair, and Cassie tapped away. And Leon was amazed, because the computer worked perfectly when she was in control. It didn't freeze once.

The more Leon thought about it, the more he thought there was something supernatural about Cassie.

After the launch party, Cassie and Leon were riding home in a taxi. Cassie was still miffed about Una taking the credit for her idea.

'Would you like me to buy you some flowers?' asked Leon.

Cassie shrugged. 'If you like.'

The taxi pulled over at a flower stall. There were buckets full of daisies and daffodils and roses, but no gerberas. This was a pity, because they were Cassie's favourite flower.

'Do you know where I could find some gerberas?' Leon asked the old lady minding the stall.

'Behind your ear,' said the old lady, who had one purple eye and one green one.

Leon pulled a bunch of bright orange gerberas from behind his ear.

'Oh, thank you very much!' said Leon, climbing back into the taxi.

'Don't mention it,' said the old lady, returning to her copy of *Witches' Weekly*. When she saw Cassie in the taxi, she waved to her and called out something about seeing her next Wednesday on Venus, but Cassie was so caught up in her own cross thoughts that she didn't respond.

Leon handed the bunch of orange gerberas to Cassie.

'I would have preferred pink ones,' said Cassie.

And the gerberas magically became pink, even though Cassie wasn't looking at them. Leon gazed out the back window and saw the old lady giving him a thumbs-up sign.

'I think we should buy a house,' said Leon.

Cassie turned to her boyfriend. 'What with?'

'Well, we might make lots of money from our new children's book.'

'And we might not,' said Cassie.

'You can't be sure of anything these days,' agreed Leon. 'Although I'm fairly sure that you're a witch. And I'd very much like to marry you and live in a house with you, not a cramped little flat.'

HOW IT ALL ENDED

It then occurred to Cassie that she hadn't been concentrating on much of the conversation.

'Leon, what did you say?' she asked.

'I'd like to live in a house with you,' repeated Leon.

'Before that.'

'I asked you if you'd like me to buy you some flowers.'

'After that.'

'Well, I did mention that you're a witch.'

Cassie tried to remain calm. 'And what makes you say this all of a sudden?'

'Well,' said Leon slowly, 'it's just occurred to me that quite a lot of strange things happen when you're around. Such as the fact that this taxi is driving all by itself.'

'You just noticed that, did you?'

'I did, Cassie, yes.'

Cassie sighed. 'And you didn't notice it the two hundred and eight other times we've taken taxis?'

'I suppose I was too busy thinking about educational things,' admitted Leon.

'Does it bother you that I'm a witch?' asked Cassie.

'Not really,' said Leon. 'Does it bother you that I'm a children's writer?'

'Of course it does!' said Cassie. 'It would bother anyone!'

'Does that mean you won't marry me?' asked Leon.

'I will have to think about it carefully,' said Cassie. 'This isn't a stupid fairytale where you can just decide to get married at the drop of a hat.'

Out on the footpath a man dropped his hat.

'I've decided,' said Cassie. 'I'll marry you. But I

want a proper wedding. With hobgoblins playing trombones and gremlins on trapezes and a million elves line-dancing and a cake.'

'Are you sure we need a cake?' asked Leon.

Cassie chuckled and hit him with the bunch of pink gerberas, and as the taxi drove off into the distance the pop music started.

The moral of this story is: You can't judge a book by its cover. Although if the cover says *Leon Stumble's Book of Stupid Fairytales*, it's a safe bet that the book will contain some stupid fairytales and a happy ending.

The End